# One Sharp Needle

## = An otherworldly love story =

*"Amor vincit omnia, et nos cedamus amori. Love conquers all things, so we too shall yield to love."* – Virgil, Eclogues.

Dear reader, this book is neither a typical love story nor a typical science fiction novel. Please adjust your expectations accordingly. Enjoy!

(C. Traven, First Edition, ©2025)

I0607781

# Contents

# 1. The Abduction

Megan was delighted with the colony. It was self-sustained and running smoothly. That was the proof of principle she had hoped for. Everyone pitched in and worked long hours to improve this place. Sure, there were some minor squabbles, but nothing too serious. Veronica, their latest arrival, was still adjusting to the new life, but Megan was confident that she would fit in eventually.

Today, they would get their 12<sup>th</sup> and final member. Mark messaged that he was waiting at the pickup location, ready to be transferred. With his exceptional computer skills, they could proceed to the next phase. Megan was excited when she saw on her laptop that the transfer was almost complete. She asked Ahmed and Jue to get Mark and carry him to the recovery room in case he was still asleep. Megan had a few other things on her to-do list today, but would give him a very warm welcome later on.

He had bought a new toothbrush from the pharmacy and some mosquito repellent from the hardware store, and also finally managed to get a much-needed haircut today. He was looking forward to four weeks of vacation at the cabin in the Sierra Mountains. The drive would be a long one tomorrow, but he didn't mind that. He would enjoy a little fishing and a lot of writing, the fresh air, the beautiful nature, and especially the tranquility away from the big, noisy city. It was early afternoon, sunny and pleasant, and the strip mall was bustling with cars and people. He walked out of the barbershop to his vehicle with the toothbrush and bug spray in his hands. When he arrived and unlocked the door, everything suddenly went black.

He woke up with a headache and a foul, metallic taste in his mouth. The room was well-lit. The bed had a firm mattress, a soft pillow, and plain, clean blankets. He was dressed in a white and gray jumpsuit. The fabric was smooth and comfortable, but the size was clearly too small for someone of his stature. He looked around and saw a bottle of water on the tiny nightstand. A simple steel table and two metal chairs were the only other furniture present. The uncarpeted floor was something like polished concrete, and the walls were made from the same brown-gray material. The ceiling also seemed to be made from the same stuff, but it emitted a slightly reddish light over its entire length. The ceiling had no airducts, and the walls had no electrical outlets or switches. The room had no windows and only one door. Next to the door, and behind a plastic curtain, was an alcove containing a sink, toilet, and a tiny shower, all made from brushed metal, possibly nickel.

He got up and walked to the door. It had no handles. He deduced that it was a door that slid inside the wall, likely powered by some form of hydraulics. Very modern, but not very safe, as someone could be crushed when the door closes. He tried to open it, but it wouldn't budge, not even a little bit.

He checked out the table. An empty glass and a pitcher of something that resembled orange juice were next to a covered dinner plate. He lifted the cover. The meal appeared to be a rather unappetizing combination of vegetables, meats, and presumably mashed potatoes with brown gravy. The dish was warm and still steaming when he removed the cover. It didn't smell much better than it looked, but it made him realize how hungry and thirsty he was. His first instinct was to sit down and devour the meal, but he decided against that. Instead, he went to the restroom to drink water from the faucet. That was actually more complicated than anticipated, since the faucet required him to continuously press a button or the water would stop. The bathroom had a small mirror. He was clean-shaven when he exited the barbershop and lost consciousness, but now noticed that his beard had grown quite a bit.

After he had quenched his thirst, he returned to the bed and sat down on its edge. How did he end up here? The last thing he remembered was pressing the remote key to open the doors of his car. Nothing after that until he woke up a few minutes ago, but obviously, several days must have passed, or his beard would not have grown so much. He speculated he had experienced a serious medical emergency in the parking lot of the strip mall and was now in some kind of hospital. However, this room lacked medical equipment, and he didn't have a vital sign monitor or an IV attached to him. He also didn't feel weak or confused, the headache notwithstanding. No, this wasn't a hospital, and the strange, locked door suggested that he had suffered a much darker fate. Before he could dwell on that any further, the door suddenly opened, and a brunette woman walked in.

He was a lousy judge of age, but he estimated that she was in her late teens or early twenties. She wore a similar jumpsuit as his and smiled broadly. Her teeth were perfect, her features symmetrical, and her body, accentuated by the tight suit, toned and very feminine.

"Hello Mark, I'm Lillian. Welcome to our little colony," she chirped.

"Ma'am, I'm not Mark. Could you please tell me how I ended up here?" he replied politely.

"Oh, you must still be confused. That happens sometimes after the transfer."

"I'm not confused, but I would like to know why I'm here."

"You are here because you wanted to join us, Mark."

"I certainly didn't and object to being held captive here."

"You can leave this room anytime."

"No, I cannot."

"Of course, you can. Just walk up to the door, and it will open for you."

He got up from the bed and walked to the door. As expected, the door did not move an inch. The woman looked at him, perplexed, but he didn't buy the feigned surprise.

"As you can see, I'm imprisoned here, but I suspect that you already knew this."

"Please wait here, Mark. I will check with the others," said the young woman and quickly exited the room again.

"I'm not Mark," he mumbled, but the girl was already out the door.

He didn't get any answers from this strange encounter but learned one crucial thing: the woman appeared only minutes after he had regained consciousness; hence, it was clear that this room was under surveillance. He tried to find the cameras, but it proved very difficult because they were integrated into the walls and ceiling. Eventually, he discovered three penny-size holes: one in the ceiling directly above the table, one in the wall facing the exit door, and one in the wall facing the bed. However, there was no surveillance in the small restroom. With nothing else to do, he sat down on the edge of the bed and waited.

# 2. Introductions

About 10 minutes later, a blonde woman stormed into the room. Just like the other lady, she was lovely and wore the same type of jumpsuit, but he could tell by her facial expression that she was quite irate. He noticed that she had turned on some device, likely a voice recorder, and that meant this room had only video surveillance, not audio.

"You are not Mark!" exclaimed the woman, demanding to know, "Who are you, and how did you get here?"

"Are you in charge here?"

"Yes, I am. Answer the question!"

"I got here because you knocked me out and abducted me in broad daylight when I tried to get into my car at the El Monte Plaza strip mall," he said calmly and added, "Now please tell me what's going on?"

"That's a lie; we didn't abduct you!" protested the woman.

"Yes, you did. Then you left me unconscious for about a week, stuffed me into this suit, and locked me up in this room."

"We didn't leave you unconscious. The transfer only takes a few hours," said the woman, and added, "The door is just malfunctioning; we would never imprison anyone."

"My beard growth contradicts: I was out cold for about a week. The door works fine, just not for me. Please don't play dumb; I'm too old for that nonsense. Just tell me what you want from me, Miss."

"Want from you?" she repeated slowly.

"If it's money, I have to disappoint you. I'm poor, but that's by choice. Also, nobody cares that I'm gone, and nobody will pay any ransom for me. I'm a lousy hostage."

"Ransom? Who do you think we are?"

"Three possibilities come to mind: a criminal outfit that takes hostages and extorts ransom is the likely one. Law enforcement, the military, or some other government organization that wants me to disappear would be my second choice, although I'm not sure whom I've pissed off enough for that. The last culprit would be some lunatic cult or religious nutcases, and these jumpsuits would fit in that picture."

"We are nothing like that."

"Whatever your intentions, you have abducted the wrong person."

"Ridiculous, the system doesn't make mistakes."

"Stay focused, lady: your intended target was someone named Mark, and we both agree that I'm not that person. Hence, you made an error," said the man, but then added more reconciliatorily, "Look, all I want is to return to where I was. So, please just let me go."

"We cannot do that."

That was not the answer he had hoped for, but of course, it made sense from the perspective of his kidnappers. He collected his thoughts for a moment before he spoke again.

"Yes, I feared that much. I have seen your face and that of your cohort earlier. I could also describe this room to the authorities. If you let me go, you could incur serious legal trouble. I would promise not to press charges, but of course, you cannot take that risk," said the man and added, "So, I shall appeal to your mercy: please kill me quickly."

"What? Kill you? Are you out of your mind?"

"I'm a rational man, and it is the logical consequence of an abduction gone awry," he said and explained, "You will get no money, and since I can identify you, you have no other choice now. So, I'm ready. Just get it over with."

"You are insane!"

"Perhaps I am? And if I am, you are either incredibly naïve or fearless, Miss. Sure, you are in excellent physical shape and about 40 years younger than me, but unarmed, and I'm about twice your weight and more than a head taller. You said you cannot let me go, so I have nothing to lose. Even at my advanced age, I could seriously injure or even kill you."

"Why haven't you?"

"Primarily because I'm not a violent person. But I also know that this prison cell is under surveillance, and as soon as I make a threatening move, your security will storm in with batons and tasers and beat the crap out of me."

"It's not a prison. Stop saying that!"

"Then what is it?"

"It's just an apartment. A comfortable, safe space for new transfers to recover. It's a little barren, but we've brought you food and drinks," said the girl, adding, "Yes, we monitor this room, but only for the safety and well-being of the new members. This place isn't anything like a prison. It's a new colony!"

"A new colony?"

"A new settlement on a different planet," said the woman, and added, "and that's the only reason why we cannot let you go. There is no way back to Earth."

"Are you really expecting me to believe that, Miss?"

"I know it sounds crazy, but I swear it's the truth."

He took a moment to study this young woman carefully. Her words sounded sincere, and her body language supported that, too. This lady firmly believed what she had just said.

"Hmm, your oath is genuine," he said, nodding.

"But?"

"It is also delusional. However, we shall continue this discussion within your reference frame now. Perhaps that will lead to better results? Just understand that it is merely an intellectual exercise."

"Alright?" wondered the woman, unsure how to take that comment.

"Why can't you send me back to Earth?"

"Because there is no physical body there."

"So, you disintegrate a body on Earth and reconstruct it here?"

"Yes, it's something like that, but we cannot do it in reverse because we don't have the alien technology on Earth," said the woman and explained, "When the body disintegrates, it is also scanned. Then, the data is transferred here, and this facility constructs a new body. We make sure that the new body is better suited for the environment, free of all genetic defects and diseases, younger, stronger, and more attractive."

"How many people do you have, and are they all enhanced like you?"

"We have 11 members, and of course, they are all like me."

He had asked that question to size up his odds of escape, but hadn't expected an accurate headcount of his abductors. These individuals were amateurs who didn't regularly take hostages. That was both good and bad: good because he might find a way to get away from these dilettantes, but also bad because his abductors would act unpredictably since they are not professionals.

"Aha, but my body is exactly the same as it was, with all the blemishes, defects, aches, and pains."

"That was not supposed to happen."

"Another mistake by the system? Just like the door that's not opening for me?"

"The door opens because a module is integrated into the base of the skull. It also helps with other things, like calculations and certain memory functions."

"You have that module, but I don't, so the door won't open?"

"Correct, but I think we can fix that. Just give us some time, please."

"Fix it? What would be the purpose of that?"

"Then you can move about the colony, of course."

"That makes no sense. You cannot integrate me into your group."

"But why not?"

"Even if I were to consent to that, I'm old, not in the best of health, beyond the age of procreation for all practical purposes, and of average intelligence. I write books as a hobby, and that's the only skill I have left. I'm not suited for a colony among the stars," he said and continued, "I will be an outcast here, living off your handouts, draining your resources, and a constant reminder of your failure, one that you would have to explain to your children as well. Worse yet, I might not be able to take care of myself in a few years because I will be too frail and possibly senile, too."

The woman didn't reply, but he sensed that she was considering his words seriously. He thought that was an encouraging sign and decided to push a little harder.

"Your reality or mine, we end up in the same place. If you cannot release me, you will have to dispose of me," said the man.

"You are suicidal and want us to do the deed for you!" exclaimed the woman.

He wasn't suicidal at all. His goal was to make these people uncomfortable and force them into decisions that they were not prepared to make, hoping they would make a mistake. If they did, he might have a chance to get out of this alive. He decided to provoke them even harder.

"Oh, far from it! I still have some unfinished business and would prefer to live out my remaining years serenely. But I'm not a fool, and I don't think you are either, despite your delusions. We both know how this must end," he said and continued forcefully, "but I have entertained your fantasies for long enough: you haven't delivered a single shred of evidence for your outlandish story, but there is plenty of proof that it's all a lie: if this were a different planet, why is gravity exactly the same as it is on Earth? Why do you sit there with a laptop that looks like something I could buy from Amazon? This apartment isn't alien either - it's a combination of a hotel, a hospital ward, and an interrogation room, and that door is remotely controlled by your cohorts, nothing more. Your so-called enhanced body could just be plain youth or the result of cosmetics and expensive plastic surgery. There is no module, no new bodies, no aliens, and no colony – just a bunch of delusional cultists who kidnapped the wrong guy!"

"You are calling me a liar without any proof!"

"The skeptic doesn't have to disprove the lies; the believer must prove them to be true. That's the first rule of critical thinking. They used to teach that in school."

"You are so cynical and condescending!" shouted the blonde.

"Lady, I only believe what is proven and provable. Everything else is hypothetical, and possibly nothing more than fairytales for children," said the man, and added, "I know that doesn't endear me to anyone because almost all people are mired in superstitions, conspiracy theories, prejudice, or religious nonsense. That's another reason why I cannot be part of your group."

The woman was furious now, got up very abruptly, and ran for the door. He shrugged his shoulders and sat down on the edge of the bed again. This conversation had been both enlightening and odd. Obviously, his captors were a delusional cult, perhaps something like Heaven's Gate. But he wasn't their desired target, and they even admitted to that. However, they still had no idea who he was, which was puzzling because he had his driver's license and credit cards with him when they took him. One look in his wallet could have told the abductors his real name. The man wondered if they had discarded all his personal possessions prematurely. Understandably, they chugged his phone, but perhaps they were so paranoid about the chips in the credit cards that they tossed his wallet, too. Still, not checking the identity of the target was a stupid move, but the woman didn't seem ignorant. She was confident, educated, and well-spoken. She even showed signs of critical thinking, and that's the bane of every cult. He concluded that he would need more interactions with these people to have a clearer picture.

He was really hungry now and tempted to eat the food that was still on the table. But he didn't want to eat it because it might be laced with drugs, something that would fit well with the cult hypothesis. He also didn't want to give his captors the satisfaction of seeing him consuming their table scraps. The man controlled his urge, ignored his growling stomach, and made himself comfortable on the bed for a nap.

# 3. Judgement

Megan had calmed down by the time she called for a meeting. The stranger had aggravated her, but now that she thought about it, his reaction was understandable. If someone had told her a story about a colony on a planet outside of the solar system, she wouldn't have believed it either. He was very tall and slender and might have been quite handsome in his youth, but now he was just a retiree in his sixties. However, Megan liked the way the stranger thought: he had an empirical mind, and that was something she could respect.

"I've reviewed all the transfer logs twice. Mark was scanned at the proper coordinates at 1:36 PM on April 21st and was fully reconstructed here exactly 6 hours later. All parameters were met without warnings or abnormal readings. Ahmed and Irina removed the body from the transfer chamber at 8:00 PM and brought him to the recovery room. He woke up at 8:15 PM, and at 8:20 PM, Lillian welcomed him to the colony," said Megan, and concluded, "However, the unknown man claimed to have been scanned about a week earlier in a parking lot of a strip mall, approximately 3 miles from Mark's designated location."

"Maybe he is still confused from the effects of the transfer?" wondered Lillian.

"Maybe, but he is definitely not Mark," contradicted Yue immediately.

"I'm pretty sure the guy somehow interfered with the transfer process," speculated Kevin.

"How can he trigger the transfer several days earlier from a different place? Why was his body not enhanced and held in the chamber for a week? That makes no sense, Kevin," said Megan.

"Who knows? Maybe he had some help?" wondered Yue.

"But he doesn't want to be here. So much so that he asks to be killed," said Irina.

"Let's not forget that this colony has immeasurable value to all governments on Earth and the private sector," said Ahmed, the unofficial head of security.

"Yes, but aside from us, nobody knows about it," replied Megan.

"Perhaps someone found out? Maybe Mark let something slip, and this guy is a spy or just the unwitting canary in the coal mine? A first test to see if we can be infiltrated?" postulated Ahmed.

"That's an alarming thought, and I really hope it's not true," conceded Megan.

"We should interrogate him thoroughly and put him through the grinder. If he knows something, he will spill it eventually," said Ahmed.

"That sounds like torture, and we won't do that," Megan stated firmly, adding, "It would be pointless too because even if he knows something and tells us, we have no way to verify it."

"We should try anyway. The guy might say something we can verify, or maybe we catch him in a lie, and then we know he's guilty?" said Jacques.

"You guys are paranoid. He probably ended up here by accident. Who would send a retiree on a spy mission?" wondered Sylvie and shook her head.

"Veronica, you watched the surveillance video and heard the recording. What did you find out about this guy?" asked Megan.

"His behavior is atypical. A hostage usually falls into one of two categories: they are either hostile and defiant, or fearful and compliant," said Veronica, and explained, "This man is unhappy with the situation but rational to a fault. He interacted with you as if you were his equal, not his captor."

"Let me just interrupt for a moment: he was right about you being fearless to meet with him without protection. Whenever one of us enters that room, we should have two additional armed people standing outside the door in case he becomes violent. Also, he should remain confined to the recovery room. We cannot risk him being anywhere near the sensitive equipment!" stated Ahmed.

"Yes, that's a good precaution. I never thought of that man as a hostage, but I guess from his point of view, he is one," conceded Megan and asked, "Is he violent, Veronica?"

"He is not violent, but I suspect he would still use violence if he thought that would set him free. However, he has remarkable self-control and is actually curious rather than threatened by this situation."

"Was he serious about us killing him?" asked Ron.

"Yes, but he would prefer that we let him go," said Veronica, and added, "Everything he said was based on logic, not anger, desperation, or the desire to die. He made assumptions, but they were rational ones with good odds of being correct."

"Did he lie about how he got here?"

"I'm a psychologist, not a lie detector, but from my experience, I believe that he did not lie, at least not on purpose."

"The guy is no dummy. When he referred to his intelligence as average, that was definitely a lie," interjected Jacques.

"Not necessarily. Our guest might consider himself average and views everyone else as inferior," said Veronica, and concluded, "Perhaps he is arrogant, but not a liar."

"Arrogant! That's it!" exclaimed Lillian and added forcefully, "That's why I hated that guy as soon as I met him. Instead of appreciating the miracle, he asks all these cynical questions. He can't be trusted and should never be one of us. He has to go!"

"Speaking of possible lies, it's unlikely that his body was stuck in the chamber for that long. After about three days, he would have died of dehydration," said Juan, the doctor of the colony.

"We know that the chamber buffers the transfer. We can scan multiple people in short succession, as we have done for Kevin, Lillian, and Ahmed, yet the new bodies always take 6 hours to form. The body is unconscious when it's finished. Some wake up right away, others remain asleep for a while longer. We remove a sleeping person from the chamber and bring them to the recovery room. However, if we didn't, the person would eventually wake up and be able to exit the pod on their own. I was the first to arrive, and that's what happened," said Megan, and speculated, "but it is conceivable that the chamber can sustain a body or keep it in suspended animation for an extended time. We never investigated that possibility, and I will have to check for it later."

"But even if everything he said is true, we have to be pragmatic. This colony is in its infant state. We do not have the resources to support random people who cannot contribute in meaningful ways. He has to go," said Kevin, and nodded.

"If he wants to die, maybe we could persuade him to take his own life?" wondered Irina.

"Suicidal people are either in deep despair or loneliness, or completely overwhelmed with the challenges in their lives, or suffer from extremely low self-esteem. This man appreciates solitude and is very confident. He is understandably concerned but not overwhelmed by this situation. He will not kill himself," said Veronica and typed something on her tablet.

"Since his body isn't enhanced, he will die anyway. The background radiation is too high for an unmodified human," said Juan, and added, "I estimate that he will only live 3 to 4 months, 6 at the most. We don't have to kill him since nature will do it for us."

"Could we protect him from the radiation?" asked Ron.

"It's in the air, the food and water, and even the building itself is slightly radioactive. It would be exceedingly difficult to create a clean room, and the man would have to remain in there indefinitely. That's not worth the effort or resources for someone that old," said Juan and shrugged.

"He doesn't look that old," said Ron.

"Too old for us," replied Juan.

"We are confronted with the first moral predicament of this colony, and your solution is to let an innocent old man die slowly and horribly of radiation poisoning?" said Sylvie with a frown.

"He's not proven innocent!" interjected Ahmed loudly, and several others nodded.

"I agree with Sylvie that we should solve the problem immediately. As the guy said, he will be dependent on our handouts and strain our resources. It is better if he dies quickly so we can transfer the real Mark, and he can help us get more of these alien devices operational," said Kevin, obviously missing Sylvie's point.

"True, but we would have to figure out what went wrong first. If we try again and don't get the right person, we might be back to square one," said Yue.

"Shouldn't we try to find a better solution? I don't want to be part of a murder," said Ron quietly.

"We all knew that we would have to make some hard decisions when we joined up. This is one of them," said Kevin, and suggested, "but perhaps we could tell our guest that we found a way to restore his body on Earth. He would probably appreciate that, and then we use the transfer chamber to disintegrate him?"

"You want to lie to him and then kill him?" asked Ron, and he shook his head.

"It's a humane solution, and quick and painless, just as he has requested," said Kevin, and added, "Then we figure out what went wrong, fix it, and get Mark."

"Mark contacted me and complained about the missed transfer. He said that it is imperative that we try again in the next few days, or he might not be able to come at all, but didn't explain why," interjected Megan.

"He was stalling for months, and now it can't go fast enough?" wondered Lillian and asked Megan, "Can we transfer him on short notice?"

"We could, but this glitch is concerning…" Megan started to reply, but Yue interrupted her.

"It is too risky. We might even kill Mark if the transfer malfunctions again, God forbid!"

"We need Mark, but I have to agree with Yue," said Kevin, and added, "Better safe than sorry."

"Yes, I agree too. We have managed without Mark for this long. We can do it for a while longer," said Megan, and added, "If everyone agrees that we hold off, I will let Mark know."

Nobody objected to that decision. The discussion stopped, and Megan called for a vote on Walter's fate. The colony voted 7 to 3 for his death, with only Megan, Ron, and Sylvie voting against it, but Veronica didn't vote. The second vote was to determine the method: Ahmed, Jaques, and Juan were in favor of death by radiation, but Kevin, Lillian, and Yue preferred a quick disintegration instead. Irina didn't care either way, and Megan, Ron, and Sylvie abstained, too, but Veronica did not vote once again.

"Veronica? You didn't vote," said Megan with a frown.

"Oh? I'm in favor of letting him die of natural causes. He is a fascinating specimen, and that would give me more time to study him," said the redheaded woman and turned her attention back to the tablet.

Megan ended the meeting and immediately returned to her room. The botched transfer was a significant setback. Without Mark, it would take her months to finish the next phase. The stranger was also a problem and would need to be handled appropriately. She was surprised that the colony was so eager to kill this man, but relieved that they didn't execute him outright. Perhaps he can still be of some use in some way?

# 4. New Insights

The next day, the blonde woman who claimed to be the leader of this outfit returned. She smiled when she entered and put a laptop on the table. Then she faced Walter and extended her hand to him.

"I'm Megan," said the woman.

"Walter," he replied and took it, but she moved in for a hug.

He was uncomfortable, but let it happen and even touched her shoulders slightly. It was surprising, but perhaps an opportunity? For a split second, Water considered overpowering the woman and using her or her dead body to open the door to his prison.

"Please play along, Walter," she whispered, then stood on her tiptoes and kissed his cheek.

Of course, Walter knew that sex was a potent and efficient tool of manipulation. Cults often used it to make new members more receptive to their agenda. He would play along for now, but only to learn more about these people. He didn't respond verbally but moved his head down to Megan's neck as if he was going to kiss it. Megan let it happen, but then backed away just enough to unzip her jumpsuit seductively. She let the fabric fall down to her ankles and embraced him again. Walter caressed her bare bottom with both hands, but suddenly, Megan rushed over to her laptop and pressed some keys. When she was done, she picked up her jumpsuit and got dressed again.

"Ah, you turned off the surveillance because you don't trust your cohorts. When they ask later, you will claim that you were intimate with me."

"Yes," replied Megan, and asked, "Walter, can we have another discussion?"

"Your reality or mine?"

"Mine, if you don't mind? You were right; I didn't provide you with any evidence to support my story. I want to correct that now."

"Alright, I'm listening."

"I grew up in the San Francisco Bay Area and got my Ph.D. from Berkeley. Then, I was a NASA scientist for many years. My group was responsible for monitoring space junk. We called ourselves the space janitors. It was not glamorous but essential work."

"Debris is hazardous during rocket launches and for satellites or space stations."

"Yes. In 2015, I detected a strange object. It was sizable but very dim and had the most unusual orbit. It didn't fit any known source, but since it wasn't a hazard, I just recorded it and forgot about it. The following year, I rediscovered the object, but its orbit had undergone significant changes. I got curious and asked a friend to ping the thing with a directional message array. The object pinged back, but it wasn't a satellite, and the signal was unusual. I spent the whole night fiddling with the array at my friend's observatory, and suddenly, something downloaded onto my laptop. I still have no idea how that was possible, nor could I make sense of the code at the time. I asked someone, Mark, to take a look, but he was confounded too because it didn't match any known programming language."

"This laptop?"

"No, its counterpart on Earth, and yes, I bought that one from Amazon," said Megan.

"Regardless of the programming language, a laptop is ultimately controlled by machine language that accesses the processor directly."

"That's correct, and I'm curious how you know that, but we don't have that much time right now. The processor was accessed as it always was, but it did things that shouldn't be possible," said Megan, and continued, "Since that night, I could communicate with the object from my laptop. In fact, the thing changed orbit again and became geostationary right above my home."

"Interesting, please continue."

"Every night after work, I spent hours trying to make sense of the strange interface and commands. I was so obsessed that my husband left me for another woman, and I didn't even care."

"That's some dedication," said Walter and chuckled.

"Eventually, I figured out that the object in orbit was a type of relay. It connected to other relays across the galaxy, and that was the proof that this was alien technology."

"Quantum entanglement, then."

"I won't ask how you know that, but we must talk more soon," said Megan, and added, "Finally, I realized that these other relays were actually planets that the aliens had visited or lived on. There were approximately 100 of them, but most were not suitable for human habitation. The aliens preferred higher gravity, warmer temperatures, drier conditions, and lower oxygen levels in the atmosphere. Only a handful of planets were acceptable to humans, and this world was one of them."

"How did you build this colony?"

"The aliens had an ingenious construction system. They dropped a big ball of something like Play-Doh on a planet, or maybe they created the ball on the surface, then used electrical currents to modulate it into any building you can imagine."

"Fascinating, but aside from the buildings, you would also need machinery, controls, and a power source. And I don't think you bought this bed and table from ET's IKEA store."

Walter intended to throw Megan off her game with that remark, but she just laughed out loud, then shook her head.

"You have a good sense of humor," she said and explained, "The reactor and essential equipment were inside the big ball already. But the furniture, the jumpsuits, and even that water pitcher are made by something we call the transmuter. We collect raw materials from the planet, feed them into the machine, and it will produce basic components; however, some assembly is still required. The food processor works similarly: we put organic materials in, and it turns them into edible items. It took me a long time to make it work for the nutritional needs of humans, and we still have to cook most of the stuff once it's produced."

"Alright, go on."

"At some point, I figured out that the relay could transfer matter from one destination to another. The original object was destroyed, but the transmuter created a perfect clone at the receiving end. The transmuter can only make inanimate objects, not living things. But I discovered that the aliens also had a transfer chamber. It worked similarly but was much more complex. A body was destroyed but scanned, and the information was sent here. Then the chamber recreated the body just as it was, but it was possible to enhance the clone and make it better than the original," said Megan, and added, "Walter, I swear I'm 49 years old."

"As I saw earlier, you are very well preserved," said Walter humorously.

"Thanks, but I know you don't really believe me," replied Megan and continued, "It took me 5 years to build this colony remotely from Earth. I had to transfer hundreds of tools, electronics, and everyday items in advance just to make it livable. Meanwhile, I looked discreetly for people who wanted to join me here. I found 10 volunteers, 11 if you count Mark."

"But?"

"But I made two mistakes. For one, I didn't realize how ancient the data from the relay had been. I estimate now that it must be at least 150,000 years old. The aliens are long gone, perhaps extinct, or have relocated elsewhere. According to the relay, this planet was a lush, green paradise, but that was thousands of years ago. Now, it is nearly frozen, has sparse vegetation, and has dangerous background radiation. I will say more about that later."

"Climate change or some catastrophic event?"

"It was caused by volcanic activity on a massive scale about 10,000 years ago. Radioactive ashes clouded the atmosphere, causing global temperatures to plummet. It's an ice age out there, and all of us are stuck inside this complex because going outside is dangerous."

"Hmm, volcanoes usually don't spew radioactivity."

"These ones vaporized a huge deposit of Cesium, Thallium, Thorium, Iodine, and a few other radioactive elements into the atmosphere. The weather did the rest and covered the entire planet with the fallout."

"A bad break. Since some of these isotopes have a long half-life, even 10,000 years might not be enough."

"That's not exactly common knowledge. Who are you?" asked Megan, looking at him.

"Your hostage. Please continue," replied Walter with a thin smile, and motioned with his hand a little.

"Fine. The other mistake was that I chose people as colonists whom I knew and liked, but didn't really consider how they would behave in a tight-knit group on a different planet. I believed in the good in them, but that was naïve," said Megan, and seemingly changed the topic when she added, "The radiation on this planet is too high for an unmodified body such as yours. Without genetic protection, you will perish in a few months."

"Ah, it will cause nausea, anemia, hair loss, edemas and tumors, eventually blindness, and finally death."

"Correct. The colony has voted to let you die of radiation poisoning. I'm so sorry, Walter!"

"You don't agree with them; therefore, you disabled the surveillance to talk to me privately."

"Yes," said Megan, and handed him a pill bottle, "please take one every day. It's an iodine supplement to protect your thyroid, but it won't stop the inevitable. However, I have a plan and will do everything in my power to save you. Please, just play along for now."

"Sure, I don't have anything else to do here," said Walter, and asked, "But I have a question: if the aliens can transport people between the stars, surely they could fix something like radiation damage, no?"

"The enhanced bodies are hardened against radiation, but the aliens didn't have any medical equipment. If we get hurt or ill, we have to rely on earthly medicine and care. That's why we needed a doctor here."

"OK, we conversed in your reality, and your story is a little more plausible now, but I still haven't seen any hard proof."

21

"Look at my laptop. The proof is right there."

"I wish I could, but you took my reading glasses when you abducted me."

"Shit! I didn't think of that, and I used to be as blind as a bat. Our new bodies have perfect vision, but yours was never enhanced. I will bring a magnifying glass next time."

"Alright, Megan. We will play your game."

"I wish it were just a game, Walter."

"You said you are 49 and lived in the Bay Area: where were you on October 17, 1989, around 5 PM?" Walter suddenly asked, looking at her expectantly.

"I was in a grocery store with my mom when the shaking started. I almost got hit in the head by a big bottle of apple juice," replied Megan after only a slight moment of hesitation.

"You passed that test, Megan. Now, it's best to get back to your friends before they get suspicious. A man of my age doesn't have the stamina to please a woman for this long," said Walter humorously, and he noticed that she blushed a little.

"Something tells me that you still could," replied Megan, blushing even more, and swiftly left the room.


A cult was still the most likely theory, but Walter noticed some inconsistencies. There were no mistakes in a cult because it existed on the premise that its members were right and the rest of the world was wrong. No cult would admit to failure because the leader was infallible. Instead, they would have told him that his real name was Mark because destiny, the aliens, God, or Santa Claus had named him that way. They would also say to him that he must forsake his worldly possessions for their supernatural cause, either to finance the day-to-day operations or to line the pockets of the leader. Hence, they definitely wouldn't have discarded his wallet.

Megan claimed to be in charge, and Walter didn't detect any signs of a lie. She was intelligent, educated, and lovely, but not particularly charismatic. She was lacking the narcissistic traits of a cult leader. Her story was most certainly delusional, but she didn't pretend to have some mysterious, superior knowledge, power, or divine calling. Cultists or religious zealots displayed that kind of condescendence regularly when dealing with non-believers. If this were a cult, Megan was middle management but not the real decision-maker. Perhaps this wasn't a cult but a political movement or terrorist organization? Mark, whoever he was, might be a government official, an important businessman, a celebrity, or a civil rights activist, and these individuals specifically wanted to capture him to maximize publicity.

Walter had to decide whether to play along or take action. A part of him was curious about these people. However, he didn't appreciate being abducted and had no desire to remain imprisoned here. A much darker part of him considered a violent escape. If Megan were the leader, she would make the perfect hostage. The door would open, but other members of the group might try to overwhelm him, and considering his advanced age, they would certainly take that chance. Therefore, it was likely that he had to kill the woman and perhaps several more to make it to freedom. Walter was fine with that option since they had already confirmed that he would die here eventually. He might perish in the escape attempt, too, but that was an acceptable risk. However, he lacked the means to even try for now. Maybe he could ask for a razor to shave his beard or some other tool that could be used as a weapon? These people weren't professionals, so they might grant his request out of ignorance. Walter decided to arm himself, but would hold off on the escape until he learned more about these people.

# 5. The Redhead

A few hours later, Walter had another visitor. The man was in his early twenties, not very tall, but looked like a bodybuilder in that tight jumpsuit. He carried a metal rod in his hand, probably as a weapon. After he entered, he kept his distance and didn't say a word. Lillian, the brunette woman from earlier, came into the room next. She talked quietly to the man for a moment, but Walter overheard her calling him Kevin. Then she picked up the food tray and pitcher from the table and exited again right away.

"You don't eat the food, so we will not serve it anymore," said the man and left without waiting for Walter's response.

Walter didn't care. He was not going to eat any of their food, and the water from the faucet was good enough to drink. He was about to take a little nap when another person entered the room. The woman was tall, toned, and voluptuous, with long, wavy auburn hair and striking emerald eyes. She turned the chair by the table to face Walter on the bed, then sat down with her legs crossed and typed something on her tablet.

"Hello. I have a few questions for you. Please answer with the first thing that comes to your mind," said the woman, and asked, "What is your favorite color?"

"I don't have one."

"What kind of music do you prefer?"

She went through a lengthy list, and Walter humored her with some answers, but most of them were either useless, cynical, or blatantly false. The woman probably knew, but didn't seem to mind. After she stopped with the questions, she spent a few minutes on her tablet again.

"Are you the interrogator?" he asked.

"Something like that," replied the woman, still busy with her device.

"You asked me a bunch of meaningless questions, but not who I am, what I do, or why I'm here. If you are an interrogator, you are doing a lousy job."

The woman placed her tablet on the table and smiled slightly.

"I didn't ask for your name because you will not give it to me."

"Well, you didn't give me yours either."

"Why don't you take a guess?"

Walter had to laugh at that and shook his head. This was bizarre, but he still thought about it for a moment.

"Valkyrie?"

"Wow, Norse mythology, and it's pretty close. Tell me how you came up with that name."

"You look Nordic, and there is a big 'V' on the back of your tablet."

"Fascinating! I like Valkyrie. Please call me that."

"OK, Valkyrie."

All the people Walter had seen so far were perfect specimens of Homo Sapiens – young, strong, healthy, and attractive. Megan had told him that the whole group was like that, and now he believed it. Were they supremacists trying to create a new master race by selective breeding? Right on cue, the woman looked at him and asked:

"I have another question: what is your sexual preference?"

"Young, tall redheads who ask too many questions. I like to punish them in bed," said Walter sarcastically.

"Kinky, and you'll get your wish someday, but not yet," said the woman quite seriously.

Walter laughed a little when he heard that, because this woman had taken flirting to a whole new level. Even if he were 40 years younger, she was clearly out of his league, and they both knew that, yet she stated that they would have sex as a matter of fact. It was so absurd that he began to wonder if he would actually sleep with her. Perhaps throwing him off his game was the intended effect?

"What's the point of all this, lady?"

"There was no point; I just wanted to meet our intriguing guest."

"Alright, you have met me. What's next?" asked Walter.

She looked at him for a good minute but didn't say a word.

"Most people are excited when they meet someone new and are eager to hear what they have to say. But you only contemplate how you would kill them if you had to do that."

"I'm a prisoner. Is that surprising under these circumstances?"

"You consider it under any circumstances," said the woman.

Walter knew that she was right. He had contemplated ways of killing every visitor to his prison, including her. But he found it interesting that she was not nervous around him at all. Perhaps she relied on security outside the door, but Walter suspected that this woman simply didn't know what fear was.

"Care for one last question?" she asked a moment later.

"If you must," said Walter, shrugging.

"Would you kill if you could escape that way?"

"If I thought that was possible, you would be dead already."

"Hmm, you could have appealed to their decency. The guilt would have made it harder for them to execute you, and they might have tried to save you instead."

Walter found it fascinating that the woman referred to the group in the third-person plural. Was she excluding herself? This was one of the oddest conversations he had had in decades, but he actually enjoyed it.

"Yes, I could have done that."

"Instead, you gave them justification to kill you. Why?"

"Rapists and murderers often justify their deeds by claiming that the victim had it coming or was asking for the bad stuff, and they just helped it along. I needed to know if your group fell into that category."

"Aha, it was a test. Now that you know that your abductors are depraved, it will dictate your response. When the opportunity arises, all of them will be dead."

"I still prefer a peaceful resolution."

"You prefer it, and that's why you cooperate with Megan instead of snapping her neck."

"It's such a lovely neck," said Walter, fully aware that his words could be seen as a potential threat to her friend, but she seemed unperturbed.

"Is it?" asked the woman and then ended the conversation, "I would love to talk to you more, but alas, it's time for Valkyrie to go. Goodbye, stranger."

She picked up her tablet, smiled at him broadly, and swiftly exited the room, but stopped again in the open doorway.

"Can you ever stop thinking?"

"What do you mean?"

"Can you stop thinking and be in the moment?"

"I'm not sure if I can. Can you?" asked Walter, but she just shook her head and was gone.

Whoever this woman was, she was no cult member but could be the true leader. There was nothing delusional about her. This visit was for a purpose, and the questions were just a distraction, but Walter had no idea what her real agenda might have been. But he sensed that Valkyrie, or whatever her real name was, liked him even if it was in a predatory sense, and he had to admit that he was intrigued by her, too. Her last question was fascinating, and he sensed that it was imperative to her, but he had no idea why. Walter concluded that the woman was a master manipulator, someone he had to observe closely.

# 6. Sabotage?

Megan dropped her laptop on the steel table. Then she hugged and kissed Walter on the lips, quickly undressed, and turned off the surveillance. It gave Walter pause. When she had done that the first time, it was justified: she got undressed while the surveillance was active, then remembered that it was still on and turned it off to have some privacy. Anyone who was watching would have thought that was a very plausible explanation. But she didn't have to do that more than once. In fact, doing it more than once would make an alert watcher suspicious because nobody is that forgetful.

So, Megan wanted someone to see that she undressed for Walter, or she wanted Walter to see her nude. Just on cue, Megan picked up her jumpsuit, and suddenly, something fell out of the pocket. Naked as she still was, she bent down to pick up, exposing her shapely rear to Walter. However, because she was quick to retrieve the item, Walter wasn't sure if it was intentional or just an accident. Still, something didn't add up here.

Walter sat down on the bed while Megan put her jumpsuit back on. After she was dressed again, she handed Walter the item she had dropped. It was a magnifying glass. Then she took her laptop and sat next to him at the end of the bed.

"Take a look, Walter."

The strange symbols on the screen reminded Walter of a mixture of Nordic runes, Egyptian hieroglyphs, Arabian script, and Chinese characters. This wasn't a known language, but of course, that wasn't evidence of extraterrestrials either. Megan scrolled through some data and graphs until she found pictures of this planet taken from orbit. It didn't look like any planet in the solar system or some elaborate artwork, but it was like the real thing. The planet was mostly covered in ice, and two small moons were circling around it. Megan selected a specific spot on the surface and showed Walter how to zoom in to see the whole complex from above. One peculiar thing was that Megan had to do some contortions with her hands to press numerous keys simultaneously. This interface was designed for someone with more fingers or perhaps more hands than a human. It wasn't the indisputable proof Walter had hoped for, but it gave a little more credence to Megan's story.

"So, where exactly is this planet?"

"We have no idea," Megan replied, laughing.

"You must have some clue?"

"None of the constellations look like what we saw from Earth, but Irina identified two stars by their spectral lines, Deneb and Betelgeuse. She triangulated them with the center of the Milky Way, and her rough estimate is that we are about 500 light-years from Earth, but with a huge margin of error."

Walter liked that answer. If Megan had given him an exact location, her story was most likely delusional because, even on Earth, it was exceedingly difficult to determine star distances accurately. It would be much harder on a world so far removed and without sophisticated astronomical tools and satellites.

"Have you figured out why the transfer failed?"

"No. Everything was exactly as specified," replied Megan.

Walter noticed that Megan was apprehensive about the transfer mishap, although she tried to hide it. Mark must be essential to her or to her agenda.

"Are you in charge of the transfer protocols?"

"Yes. While a few of us have learned the basics of the alien code, only I do the transfers."

"But some of your friends could theoretically do it, too?"

"Kevin, Irina, Yue, Veronica, and maybe Ahmed have a basic understanding of the interface, but probably not enough to do it right."

"Megan, have you considered sabotage?"

"Sabotage? Why in the world would anyone sabotage us?"

"Hmm, maybe someone doesn't like Mark and didn't want him here? Or someone needed the system to fail to create a crisis, and then use that to supplant you as the leader?" speculated Walter and added, "It is also conceivable that someone wanted to transfer a different person instead of Mark – a lover maybe – but they were not skilled enough and got me instead? Or maybe someone just wanted you to fail out of spite?"

"Scary thoughts, Walter."

"Megan, I don't know anyone in your colony, and how you relate to each other. But if they have no scruples letting me die a slow, painful death, you should prepare yourself for other unpleasant surprises."

"But they were nice, rational people back on Earth."

"Unless you can observe their behavior in an extreme situation, you will never know somebody completely. A colony on a different world is as extreme as it gets. The brave ones become cowards, the smart ones devolve into imbeciles, and the principled transform into brutal savages, or vice versa. You can rarely predict that beforehand."

"But most of the time, we are not faced with extreme circumstances."

"Under mundane conditions, anyone can pretend to be anything. It's easy, and we all do it. But when the gloves are off, the true character comes to light," said Walter, but Megan didn't seem to like that comment.

"Kevin is my ex. We made up and are friends now. He was eager to join me here and even brought his new wife, Lillian, along, but I know he still harbors some resentments. Ahmed is Kevin's buddy, a former military man, and his primary concerns are safety and security; however, he tends to follow orders blindly. Irina is a bit of a mystery. She is an astronomer, and I have known her for 20 years, but I don't know much about her. I was surprised when she asked to be part of this project. Yue was in my group at NASA. She is usually a nice person, but quite temperamental. Sometimes, I worry that she might have some issues, but Veronica is taking care of her now."

"Veronica?"

"She is my therapist."

"You asked your therapist to join you among the stars?" asked Walter, and he raised his eyebrows.

What a strange twist! Many people need therapy at some point in their lives, but he couldn't imagine that anyone would take their therapist on a one-way trip to another planet. Veronica must be more than just a counselor. Perhaps a close friend, a relative, or a lover?

"Look, I have OCD and some inhibitions. She helped me a lot with that."

"She decided to join her patient on another world?"

"She said she had nothing to lose," said Megan, and added with a sigh, "but Veronica wasn't a good choice from the beginning."

"Why?"

"She is extremely smart, competent with her analysis, and her advice is spot on. But she has no compassion and tends to rub people the wrong way with her brutal honesty."

"Not a therapist, but a psychopath?"

"I like Veronica, and I'm grateful for her help, but you might not be that far off," admitted Megan.

"Oh, she is one. I've met her already."

"Veronica was here?" asked Megan, surprised.

"Yes, she asked me a bunch of questions and made me guess her name. I didn't guess right and called her Valkyrie. She thought that was fascinating."

"That sounds like her, but I had no idea," said Megan, and asked, "So, which one is the saboteur?"

"Do all of them know Mark?"

"No, only Kevin and Yue know him."

"And how do they feel about the guy?"

"Kevin might still be jealous because I had a brief fling with Mark in college, but Kevin is jealous of every man, even though we have been divorced for 5 years and he has a new wife."

"Hmm, he paid me a visit after our fake lovemaking. I could sense the animosity."

"Kevin was here, too?"

"Yes, he told me that you would no longer deliver food since I'm not eating it."

"Geesh! He is such a bastard. I will fix that later."

"You said that Yue knows Mark, too?"

"She met Mark through me, and I think they had an affair at some point, but it ended a long time ago."

"If it ended badly, she might not want to see him again."

"She never told me how it ended," said Megan, and shrugged before she continued, "Veronica hasn't met Mark, but we've talked about him in our sessions. Irina and Ahmed don't know him at all. That's why they had no idea you were not Mark when they retrieved your body from the transfer chamber."

"That makes sense," said Walter, and added, "In the order of likelihood, your saboteur is Kevin, Yue, Veronica, Irina, or Ahmed."

"I understand why you have Kevin and Yue at the top of the list, and I agree. But explain the order after that."

"If Veronica is a psychopath, she has her own agenda, and that's almost certainly not yours. You don't know much about Irina and were surprised by her joining, which means she also has an unknown goal. If Ahmed likes to follow orders, who ordered him to be here?"

"Good points."

"Tell me about the other cultists," said Walter with a smirk.

"They are not cultists!" stated Megan firmly, but then elaborated, "Sylvie is my niece and about as old as she looks. She suffered from an aggressive, debilitating disease. By the time she joined, she was already bound to a wheelchair. Ron is her boyfriend. They met in high school, and he stuck with her despite her condition and his strict, religious parents. Juan is our doctor and a friend of Ron's, but I don't know much about him."

"Lillian is Kevin's new wife, and you met her when you woke up. I don't think she likes me very much, but she has been helpful to the colony. Jacques is Lillian's younger brother. He is the cocky type, but hasn't done anything wrong, as far as I know. However, he seems to have trouble accepting guidance from women. As I mentioned earlier, Mark is a college acquaintance and an outstanding programmer. He was supposed to help me with the alien code."

"Did you all arrive at the same time?"

"No, Sylvie and I were the first to transfer a year ago. About two months later, Irina joined us. Ron wanted to come with Sylvie, but had to work it out with his family first. Ron and Juan got here about a month after Irina. Yue was next, and then about 4 months ago, Kevin, Ahmed, and Lillian joined. Lillian begged me to let her little brother come too, and we transferred Jacques about 2 months later. Veronica was the last to arrive, only a month ago. Mark was supposed to be here last year, but kept stalling for the longest time. However, he was recently eager to come as soon as possible. I'm not sure what has changed, but we need him and his computer skills."

"Megan, you said you had a plan?"

"I told you that the relay data was ancient, but I was able to update it last night. I found one planet decently suited for humans: located in a stable star system, it has a temperate climate, a quiet geology, is not too dry with sufficient oxygen, but it is bigger than Earth and has 1.3 G. You will definitely feel the difference."

"You want to send me there?"

"Yes, I will tell the colony that you requested a quick end to save us resources. They will likely go for that. You will be disintegrated, but instead of dying, your body will be recreated on the new planet, this time with all the enhancements."

"Interesting, and assuming that this isn't a giant hoax, it could work."

"I swear it's not a hoax, but you would be all alone on that new world."

"I can handle that, Megan."

Megan didn't say anything for a while. She stared at the back of her hands with a worried facial expression. Eventually, she sighed and looked at him again.

"Walter, I have to remotely build a complex first and stock it with some items you cannot make with the transmuter. I have to use the relay to steal them from Earth."

"Steal them?"

"Yes, the relay requires a line-of-sight. It can only disintegrate and scan items that are out in the open. I could transfer a patio table on a deck, but not a dining table inside a house," said Megan, and added, "I have to look around my old neighborhood and see if my neighbors have left some useful stuff in their gardens or driveways. It's tedious and hit-and-miss."

"How did you get all the equipment you needed for this colony?"

"I bought it, placed it on my patio, and zapped everything from flashlights to laptops," said Megan, and concluded with a deep sigh, "Constructing the new complex and making it livable won't take 5 years again because I've learned how to do it, but it will still take a lot of time."

"Time that I don't have because of the radiation."

"Sadly, yes."

"If you transfer me when I'm already dying, can I still be restored on the other end?"

"In theory, you could be restored, but you would suffer tremendously until that time."

"Then that's the only option. You work as fast as you can, and I try to hang in there for as long as I can."

"Walter, if you want to do that, you need to eat, and I will get you some supplements too."

"Maybe I have a bite just to piss off your ex," quipped Walter.

"Yes, piss him off. Kevin is an ass!" replied Megan and laughed out loud.

"OK, lover. Time for you to go," said Walter.

"If you flirt with me like that, one of these days, I might not put my clothes back on," said Megan, and she blushed.

"Well, that gives me some incentive to stay alive," Walter said with a smile, but added more seriously, "Thanks for your efforts, Megan."

It had been an interesting conversation today, but Megan had not delivered enough evidence to convince Walter of anything. There was also another inconsistency: Megan claimed that this planet was in an ice age, and that picture from orbit seemed to corroborate that. If that was indeed true, it should have been a priority to find a better home many months ago. It didn't make sense to him that she waited until now to update the relay data. More likely, she already knew about this better planet, but, for some reason, did not want to relocate the colony there.

Walter knew that the adverse health effects didn't have to be the result of radiation. They could be chemically induced by lacing the food or water with compounds that mimic the effects. Walter wasn't sure why they were poisoning him when a knife or a bullet could do the job much faster. The room was under constant surveillance, so perhaps they liked to watch him suffer?

But that seemed to contradict Megan's conduct: while the flirting was obviously just meaningless banter, Megan was objectively friendly to him. There was no need to convince Walter of anything, since they had already planned his demise. Why was she wasting her time? Was she simply trying to keep him compliant? Was it guilt, or did she have a very different agenda?

35

Lastly, Megan didn't seem overly concerned about a possible saboteur, yet she obviously didn't trust her group, or she wouldn't have disabled the surveillance every time she talked to him. Walter found that to be contradictory, but had no reasonable explanation for that inconsistent behavior.

# 7. Breaking Ground

It wasn't a rule but a tradition that the colony always met for dinner. The group also celebrated Sylvie's 22nd birthday today, and Lillian had made a cake. They cut the cake, cheered for Sylvie, and while they were eating, Kevin suddenly asked with a smug grin:

"Do you guys know that Megan is sleeping with our prisoner?"

Of course, Megan knew that was coming sooner or later. Ahmed had insisted that someone was always outside the door to Walter's room when she visited. They knew when Megan entered and when she left. They also knew that the surveillance was turned off for about an hour whenever Megan was with Walter.

"Eww, gross!" exclaimed Yue, and even Sylvie looked shocked.

"I would rather be dead than sleep with someone that old," added Lillian and made a face.

"He is not much older than we are," countered Megan quietly.

"I bet he can't even get it up anymore," quipped Kevin, and Jacques laughed out loud.

"ED is common in men of his age," noted Juan.

"It's none of your business, but he's doing just fine," said Megan.

"After you sucked him for an hour?" asked Kevin facetiously, and Jacques laughed even louder.

"You are vulgar, Kevin!" yelled Megan angrily, and she wanted to say more, but Veronica interrupted.

"We are all concerned that our guest could be an infiltrator. However, you can reach the truth more easily and reliably with deception and persuasion rather than brute force. Megan's approach is effective."

"That... actually makes sense," said Ahmed and nodded.

"Bah, Megan would never sleep with anyone she doesn't like," insisted Kevin.

"Megan puts the colony above everything else. You, of all people, should know that, Kevin," said Veronica and smiled at him sweetly, but Kevin looked furious and didn't reply.

"Keep us updated if you find out something. If we have a leak, we must plug it!" stated Ahmed.

"Yes, I will," said Megan, then left the common area and retreated to her room.


Megan started the final phase of the project the next day, before anyone was even awake. Without Mark, it would take considerable time and effort. She looked at her old notes and decided to build the new complex exactly like this one. It was not ideal, but it would save her some time. For a while, she was silently engrossed in the work, but suddenly, there was a knock on the door.

"Meg, are you awake?" hollered Veronica from outside the room door.

"Morning, V, come in!"

The tall woman entered with two cups of hot coffee, or what passed for coffee on this world. She sat down next to Megan and studied the laptop screen. Megan fought the urge to close the program because Veronica was sharp and would notice that Megan was hiding something.

"Are you redesigning our building? I want a room with a big window this time."

"I'm experimenting with the layout, but it's not that easy. The aliens were much smaller than we are and didn't have straight walls, stairs, or windows in their houses. They didn't even have lights and must have lived in dark burrows or hives."

"That sounds like a lot of work. No wonder it took you so long to build this place."

"Yeah, I'm not an architect. I had to start over many times."

"Oh? You can reset it?"

"Yes, that's actually a big advantage of this building. We don't need to do any demolition because the big ball is the default, and it will always go back to that."

"That building on the screen is still mostly a ball. Is it a simulation?"

"Something like that. I was just playing around with it," lied Megan.

Megan didn't want to reset the building because that meant that she would lose a few hours of work, but if Veronica thought this was just a simulation, it was best to keep her unaware. She pressed a series of keys in quick succession to initiate the reset, and Veronica was paying close attention to everything Megan was doing on the computer. The screen showed how the unfinished building distorted and contracted on itself.

"You see, now it reverts back to the default. It takes just a few minutes."

"Fascinating. Does everyone have to be out of the building when you do that?"

"Oh yes, anything other than the built-in machinery will be crushed. That's why I can't just reset the complex and start over with a better design."

"Makes sense, and I should really learn more about this alien tech," said Veronica, adding, "Drink your coffee, Meg."

"Thanks, V," said Megan and sipped from the cup before she asked, "Do you really think we should let Walter die?"

"Something like that was bound to happen sooner or later. It's a waste because Walter is brilliant and educated. He could contribute here, but he is old, and nothing will stop the radiation. We will study him until the end. Perhaps we can learn something useful from this unfortunate situation?"

Megan didn't reply, but restarted the alien construction program. Veronica looked at the screen and massaged Megan's shoulders. Megan liked that and smiled at her.

"How's the sex with Walter?" asked the redhead and grinned at her.

"Better than expected," lied Megan.

"Ah, a lifetime of experience. I envy you, Meg."

"Yeah, something like that," mumbled Megan.

"The young studs are good for a hard quickie, but the older guys know what makes a woman tick," said Veronica, and added softly, "Don't mind Kevin and the others. They are just jealous."

"You are strange today, but thanks for defending me last night. I don't sleep with Walter because I want to find out his secrets, but…"

"…but you want to give the condemned man one last cigarette before the execution. That's very noble of you, Megan."

"Yes, I think that's it," said Megan.

"Good, I support that," said Veronica, softly touching Megan's shoulder, and added, "Enjoy, but be very careful with Walter. He isn't an infiltrator, but he is not some random retiree either."

"Do you want to elaborate, or should I guess?"

"He is like me," said Veronica simply and ended the conversation: "Ok, I'll let you fiddle with the Play-Doh. See you for lunch, Meg."

After Veronica left, Megan just stared at the screen of her laptop for several minutes. Veronica's cryptic comments were odd, but Megan was confident that she could handle Walter. He was intelligent and skeptical, but not a real threat to her or to the project. A decision slowly formed in her mind, and it made her smile a little. Then she finished her coffee and restarted the construction on the new planet. There was much work to be done!

# 8. Appearances

After several days of not visiting him, Megan entered the room. She went through her usual routine while Walter was stretched out on the bed. He was going to get up, but she pushed him down onto the pillow and then put her naked body on top of his. She kissed him several times before finally getting up again and turning the surveillance off. She took her time to get dressed and didn't even zip up her jumpsuit completely before she sat down next to him on the edge of the bed. She was typing something on her computer, and Walter sat up, using the magnifying glass to take a look.

"So, the alien technology can scan humans, transfer them here, and not only assemble them correctly but also enhance them?" asked Walter as he studied her work.

"Heaven's no! The technology was meant for alien bodies, not ours."

"Then how did you get it to work?"

"The relay had scanned humans when it arrived in orbit and added the information to its database. I found the data and modified it, but I almost made a serious mistake. The relay had scanned 4 different humanoids: us, the Neanderthals, the Denisovans, and Homo Erectus. That's how I know that the relay has been in orbit for hundreds of thousands of years."

"Interesting."

"I actually edited the Neanderthals, not us. Luckily, I noticed my mistake, or all the colonists would look a little different now."

"What did you edit?"

"I'm not a geneticist, and even if I were, I probably would have failed. However, the alien program has an amazing feature: it can visualize genetic changes in any living organism and displays a table with all the important parameters. After I entered the basic genetic profile, it was a lot like creating an avatar for a video game."

"So, you used the original DNA of your colonists?"

"Yes, that was the starting point. Then I added all the necessary changes and modified their appearance."

"Ah, eugenics."

"No, of course not. I followed the specifications of our future colonists to the letter. When they approved, I locked in the profile, and the transfer chamber did the rest."

"Do your friends look like they did on Earth?"

"Juan and Lillian look very different, but the rest resemble their old selves," said Megan, and added quietly, "more or less."

"Ah, let me guess: all the women wanted to lose weight and have shapely figures, and all the men wanted more muscles and a bigger...well, you get the idea."

"Do you blame them?" she asked and blushed.

"Oh, of course not. In society, appearance is critical, second only to wealth, and far ahead of intelligence, a good personality, or hard work. If you are pretty or rich, you can be lazy, an asshole, and dumb as rocks, yet still have a great life," said Walter, but Megan didn't seem to like that comment.

"I changed my appearance," admitted Megan, but added quickly, "but you would still recognize me on Earth."

"You look lovely, Megan," said Walter, and asked, "You said that a person will be rebuilt in the transfer chamber, but other stuff just comes out of the transmuter. Obviously, they must be similar?"

"They are similar, yet very different. The transfer chamber must accurately recreate complex proteins and nucleic acids without error. Any mistake and the person will be deformed or even dead. The transmuter doesn't care about small mistakes – a wrench is still a wrench even if some atoms are out of place. That's why the transfer takes hours, but zapping an object can be done in a few minutes."

"A good explanation," said Walter, and asked, "It is not impossible, but highly unlikely that the transfer chamber creates matter directly from energy. Hence, the machine must have a supply of ingredients to clone the body. Where does that come from?"

"Excellent question, Walter. Perhaps some reservoir inside the building?"

"The transmuter also recreates items seemingly out of thin air when something is transported here. But you told me that you have to add raw materials to it if you want to make something new and specific like this table."

"Correct, and the food processor also works the same way, but I have no explanation."

"You admit that you don't know the answer instead of trying to feed me some bullshit. That gives you more credibility, Megan," said Walter with a little smile.

"Thanks, I guess."

Suddenly, Walter had to laugh out loud and didn't stop for a while. Megan looked puzzled at him, almost fearing that the old-timer had lost his mind.

"I believe I know how it works, but you might not like it," said Walter, still chuckling.

"Tell me!" insisted Megan loudly.

"There is a reservoir of ingredients. It's called your sewer system and waste disposal. That's where the chamber gets the resources to make a new body."

"Oh, my goodness!" exclaimed Megan in shock.

"Yep, we are literally full of shit," quipped Walter, and Megan couldn't stop laughing.

For a while, they enjoyed the good humor and said nothing else. Eventually, Megan got serious again and asked:

"Do you believe now, Walter?"

"You have provided some evidence for your story."

"But not enough. What can I do to convince you?"

"You could take me outside and let me have a look at this planet. If I see two moons in the sky, it would go a long way."

"I'm so sorry, but I can't do that. The colony voted to keep you imprisoned until you die."

"But you are the leader. Surely, you could take me out there for a few minutes?"

"I'm the leader, but we are a democracy, and I want to respect that," said Megan, and added, "It wouldn't help much either. The sky is almost always hazy and clouded, and the landscape is snow-covered with a few patches of barren ground. At most, you can marvel at the moss and lichen-like vegetation on some of the bigger rocks. Plus, it's bitterly cold out there. It looks a lot like Greenland and is hardly convincing."

"Do you have a taser, a Tesla coil, an arc welder, or maybe just a piezo lighter?"

"Maybe, but I would have to check the inventory. Why do you want that?"

"You said that the building is keeping its shape because of an electrical charge. Any of these devices could temporarily alter or disrupt that electric field. If you apply it to a wall in this room, and the texture changes, that would be a strong indication that the material is indeed extraterrestrial."

"That's ingenious! I will see if I can find something like that," said Megan happily.

"Good, I also have an idea how to speed up the process on the new planet."

"Tell me!" said Megan excitedly.

"Can you access the internet from here?"

"We have sent text messages and emails, but I've never tried to surf the web. I think the relay could do that."

"That sounds promising. If you zap a container, will the content be transferred?"

"Yes, I have done that before."

"Alright, just order everything you need online, have it delivered, and zap the packages. Be your own porch pirate, and let your neighbors keep their junk," said Walter, and he grinned at her.

"That's a fantastic idea, and it would save a lot of time," said Megan, but then shook her head and added, "I don't have a house on Earth anymore or a bank account."

"Too bad, I live in an apartment now, and all the packages are delivered to the lobby where the relay can't see them," said Walter, and asked, "Do you trust any of the other colonists?"

"Only Sylvie, since she is my niece, but she doesn't have a home anymore either, and Ron used to live with his parents."

"Hmm, your therapist?"

"Veronica still has her office, as far as I know. She might do it too, but can we trust her?"

"Not really, but we might not have to. Just tell Veronica that you have to get some stuff for this colony."

"I don't like to get her involved, but it's worth a shot. Maybe I can zap a few things for this place and then transfer the rest to the new planet?"

"Yes, that keeps the suspicions down," said Walter, and changed the topic: "You said Cesium and Thallium isotopes were part of the radiation hazard. Please get something called Prussian Blue. It's just a dye, but it binds to those metals and flushes them from the body."

"You are definitely a scientist. Why don't you want to tell me more about yourself?"

"Megan, I like you, but you are still my captor," replied Walter and revealed, "I was a scientist in another life, and that's all I will say. Please get the dye because it will buy me a few more days."

"I promise, I will do that," said Megan, and asked, "How are you feeling?"

"Sluggish and nauseous at times, but still fairly alright," said Walter and asked, "Can you get me some cheap reading glasses and a few books while you are zapping stuff?"

"Of course! What kind of books?" she asked as she got up from the bed.

"Maybe some on cults?" quipped Walter and added, "Anything will do. It's boring in this room."

"I'll find something for you," said Megan and left the room.

It has been another interesting interaction today. Clearly, Megan's show was intended for whoever was watching the surveillance. It could be to spite someone like her ex or to turn someone on. But whom? When Walter asked to see the planet, Megan deferred to the democratic decision of the colony. That was questionable and most likely just an excuse to keep him in this room. If she didn't want to take him outside, not even briefly, that was a strong indication that her whole story couldn't hold up. The other noticeable piece of information was that Megan had brought her therapist with her to the stars, but now she didn't trust her? There was something else going on between her and Veronica.

Megan dropped off a few of her astrophysics books the next day, but she hadn't gotten reading glasses yet. Instead, she left the magnifying glass with him. Even though reading with the magnifying glass was a little tedious, Walter was appreciative since his days had been utterly boring without any distractions in this prison.

A day later, Veronica stopped by with a pair of reading glasses and a psychology book. After another playful round of flirting, she told him to read the chapters on schizoid personality disorder and antisocial personality disorder, and he had a pretty good idea why she suggested those topics.

# 9. Surprise!

Megan looked tired when she entered Walter's room two days after her last visit. She put the laptop on the table and typed in some commands. Then she got undressed, hugged and kissed Walter, as she had been doing in the previous few meetings. But Walter realized that Megan had already disabled the surveillance, so there was no need for this deception anymore. Right on cue, Megan unzipped Walter's jumpsuit and kissed him deeply.

"Hi there, lover," said Megan and smiled at him broadly.

"You weren't joking the other day," replied Walter in surprise.

"I worked all night and need a break. Let's enjoy this."

"Oh, I will, and I hope you will too."

Lovemaking was enjoyable for Walter, and apparently for Megan as well. She was engaged and responsive, and intimacy didn't feel staged or unnatural, but it was a little strange. Megan claimed to be 49, and while that was still young compared to him, the age difference wasn't really unusual. But, of course, she looked much younger, and he dearly hoped that she was of legal age. Then again, it was also very flattering, and he resolved not to worry about it. They extended it for quite a while, took little breaks, and then continued. The pauses actually heightened the experience and led to a very satisfying conclusion for both of them. Afterward, Megan was lying in Walter's arms, softly caressing his chest.

"Do you have any new symptoms yet?"

"I have constant headaches and spat out some blood when I woke up."

"That's terrible, and I'm so sorry."

"Yes, it's not fun, but in a way, it's evidence too. You didn't lie about the radiation. Unless you are holding me at a nuclear waste dump, it gives more credence to your story."

"You still don't believe me?"

"Megan, look at the world: there is misinformation everywhere, and lies are the new truth. People believe in the most ridiculous and obscure nonsense because they have lost the ability to think critically. Education has been sabotaged to the point that it fails miserably to enlighten people. Everything is a conspiracy these days, and when it's debunked, that's a conspiracy, too. Do you really blame me for being skeptical?"

"No, I guess I don't."

"I have withdrawn because all the bullshit and all the stupid people frustrate me too much. I cannot change the world; hence, I chose solitude so I don't have to deal with it anymore."

"Now that you say that, it's one of the reasons why I wanted to be away from Earth, too. I dreamt of a better world and worked so hard because I didn't want to face everything that's wrong with humanity."

"Yeah, I tried to drown myself in work, but that wasn't very successful or satisfying. Now I write books that nobody buys or reads, but it helps me with my frustrations."

"I will read your books," said Megan, and asked, "Walter, you will have your solitude on the new planet. Would you mind if I joined you there someday?"

"If I'm still alive and it all works out, you are welcome to stop by, Megan," Walter replied, kissing her head.

"Thanks," said Megan with a big smile.

"Do you just appear to be a young adult, or has your body been fully restored to that biological age?" he asked, and noticed that Megan tensed up.

"Are you feeling old?" asked Megan quietly.

"I do, but it's not that. You said the other day that most of the colonists are around your age."

"Yes, Kevin and Ahmed are a few years older than me, and Mark is too. Lillian, Yue, and Irina are in their 40s, Juan, Jacques, and Veronica are in their mid-thirties, and only Ron and Sylvie are as young as they look," said Megan, and added, "To answer your question: our bodies were fully restored, and all the women are fertile regardless of their true age."

Sleeping with his kidnapper could have legal consequences. If he impregnated Megan, he would be financially responsible for the child, and duress would not be an excuse. It was serious, but the odds were low, so Water decided to make light of it.

"Ah, will you have my baby now?" teased Walter, raising his eyebrows.

Megan blushed and looked at him in horror. He could tell that she was very uncomfortable and regretted making that comment. But since Megan wasn't shy and quite liberated in bed, he found her reaction charming, but a little odd.

Walter ended the conversation, caressed Megan's breasts ever so softly, and blew gently in her ear. Megan couldn't help but moan loudly. He chuckled a little, then ran his tongue up and down her neck, and she thought she would climax again just from that touch alone, but Walter suddenly stopped. Megan was surprised and looked at him with a pout.

"We'll do more of that on the new planet. But we have been at it for hours, and it's time for you to go."

"Oh my, yes! Thank you for this, Walter," said Megan, then kissed him on the cheek, jumped out of bed, and promised, "I won't let you down."

Megan got dressed very quickly, but then stopped and procured something from the pocket of her jumpsuit. She handed the item to Walter, and he looked at it curiously.

"Try it," said Megan with a big smile, and ran out the door.

Walter examined the round metallic disk. The zipper of his jumpsuit was attracted by the object. Walter concluded that it must be a strong neodymium magnet. He walked over to the nearest wall and placed the item flat against it. The wall started to change, and ripples formed about as wide as a dinner plate. Walter could push the magnet about an inch into the wall as if it were a thick fluid. He pulled it back, and the wall immediately solidified again. To the best of his knowledge, no material on Earth could do that.

"The magnetic field disrupts the electric current. You are a smart girl, Megan," he mumbled and sat down on the bed.

At first, Walter suspected that he was being fooled by some kind of magic trick. He repeated the experiment several times on different walls, as well as on the floor and ceiling of his prison. Every time, the effect repeated, but the magnetic disk had no impact on the table or the chairs. Walter was genuinely shocked that Megan's outlandish claims could actually be valid. Until then, he had considered her story to be a very elaborate hoax. However, he was pleasantly surprised that she had not lied to him, as he had started to like Megan. But of course, if the story were true, that also meant that he would die painfully from the radiation. However, he didn't mind it that much anymore because learning the truth was almost worth it.

The lovemaking had been almost as shocking as the effects of the magnet on the walls: it was simply preposterous that such a young and attractive woman would voluntarily sleep with someone as old and ill as he was, even if she was much older than her looks suggested. It was not attraction or affection, so what was it?

# 10. Jealousy?

A few hours later – it must have been in the middle of the night - the door unexpectedly opened. Walter woke up and sat up on the edge of the bed. He was only in his underwear when Veronica entered the room. She walked to the table with a noticeable swing in her hips, and Walter saw that her jumpsuit was unzipped down to almost her belly button, exposing much of her ample bosom. She smiled at him and licked her lips. Walter had to chuckle and slightly shook his head before he said:

"Hello again, Valkyrie."

"Aww, that doesn't work with you," replied Veronica with a bit of a pout and zipped up her suit before she asked, "By now, you know my real name, yet you still call me that?"

"I believe you like that name, and it matches you," said Walter, and asked, "So, more useless questions tonight?"

Veronica smiled a tiny bit, and Walter knew that he was right about the name: she really liked it. The tall woman sat down, crossed her long legs, and put her tablet on the table.

"I'd enjoy listening to your witty answers again, but that's not why I'm here."

"Then why are you here?" Walter wondered, looking at her expectantly.

"I want to know how you feel about Megan."

"Ah, the sex."

"Yes, the sex. Do you like Megan, or are you using her to get out of here?" she asked bluntly.

"Maybe I just like to have some fun before I die?"

"You have unusual priorities. You don't care about rich or poor, pretty or ugly, good or evil, or any of the other stuff that humans usually worry about. You are like Sherlock Holmes, and only the truth matters to you. We have that in common, so be truthful with me."

Walter had to admit that Veronica was exceedingly observant and an exceptional judge of character. It was no surprise to him that Megan had chosen her as her therapist. He contemplated his next words for a moment and elected to be completely honest with the redheaded woman.

"I like Megan. I'd like to have some fun and would appreciate my freedom. All three statements are true."

"Would you sleep with me, too?" Veronica asked, changing the focus of the discussion.

"Is that an offer?"

"Not yet, but answer the question."

"Under the right circumstances, I would sleep with you, but I doubt that you would sleep with me."

"Why do you say that?"

"I have my reasons."

"Fine, but your doubts are misplaced. That's all for now," said Veronica, and asked, "Will you keep my visit between us?"

"Yes," said Walter, asking with a thin smile, "Do you enjoy watching the surveillance when Megan is here?"

It gave her pause, only for a split second. But it was enough for Walter to know that Megan's show was most likely for Veronica, not to piss off Kevin. Veronica got up from the table. She approached him and traced the long scar on his left shoulder with two fingers. Her touch was soft and almost sensual.

"The scar. Will you tell me about it?"

"It was the result of an accident a long time ago," he replied, but she looked at him as if she didn't believe it.

"Goodbye, Walter," she said, turned around, and left the room without another word.

Megan and Walter had pretended to be intimate for over three weeks now, yet Veronica showed up only when they actually had sex. The surveillance was off, so the most likely explanation was that Megan had told her therapist about it as soon as she had left. But Walter didn't buy it: Megan wasn't a gossip girl, and she didn't seem to trust Veronica very much. Perhaps Veronica was so observant that she had noticed subtle changes in Megan's behavior? That was a more likely explanation, but why did that prompt the redhead to stop by in the middle of the night? Veronica was brilliant but not very personal. It seemed unlikely that she was genuinely concerned that Walter was taking advantage of her patient.

The fact that Megan had slept with him was scarcely believable, considering that there were several younger, healthier men available. So, it appeared to be even more far-fetched to think that Veronica, as beautiful as she was, would be jealous of Megan. Could Veronica be jealous of Walter? Was Megan intentionally fueling that jealousy?

Playing the seductress was a charade, and Veronica knew that it wouldn't work. Walter wasn't sure why she even tried that unless she thought of it as a joke, and in all fairness, it did make him chuckle. But when they were talking about intimacy, two of Veronica's words got stuck in Walter's mind: not yet. Walter's days were clearly numbered now, so what did she mean by that?

Lastly, she asked Walter to keep her visit confidential, which was interesting in several ways. Was she concerned that Megan found out or that the other colonists discovered her interactions with him? Or was it a test of sorts? Without a doubt, Veronica was a mysterious figure with a complex personality, but it was unclear whether she was a formidable adversary or an unexpected friend.

# 11. Colony Issues

It was midmorning, and Megan had left the room door open to air out her quarters. The complex didn't have vents, so rooms tended to get stuffy over time. She was working diligently on Walter's new home when Veronica walked in.

"Meg, we have to talk," said Veronica, peeking over Megan's shoulder.

"Sure, V?" said Megan, closed the laptop, and looked at the redhead.

"Sexual interactions are important for humans."

"Uhm, I suppose so?"

"How did you envision that to work out for this colony?"

"Well, Kevin has Lillian, and Sylvie has Ron…," replied Megan, but trailed off because there were only two couples on this planet.

"And all the other people just miraculously match up with each other? Admit it, you didn't think about it at all."

"No, I didn't. Is it really a big problem?"

"It's a huge problem for morale and happiness on Earth, but here, it's crucial since we have to reproduce, or this place will go extinct."

"I guess that's true," said Megan, and sighed, "What can we do?"

"Do you like Walter?"

"I think I like him."

"I like him, too. Would you share him with me?" asked Veronica bluntly.

"Uhm, that's a little weird coming from you, and he is dying anyway…"

"But if he weren't, would you share him with me? Would you be willing to sleep with both Ahmed and Jacques if they can't find mates? Or share Ron with Sylvie? Or sleep with Mark again if he ever joins? Or Kevin?"

"Definitely not Kevin!" protested Megan, and she was about to go off on that tangent, but Veronica waved her off.

"Focus and be honest: could you do any of that because you might have to, or the colony goes to hell in a hurry."

"I suppose if the colony's existence depends on it, I might be able to do it. Could you do it, V?"

"I could sleep with Walter and maybe even enjoy it. I could sleep with all the other guys, too, but refuse to do that, as you know."

"I think I could share Walter with you, maybe share Ron with Sylvie, even if he is not my type, but it wouldn't be easy for me. I guess I'm too old-fashioned."

"It's a scientific fact that humans are not monogamous. But it's a societal fact that they must pretend to be monogamous. Hypocrisy or not, most people cannot unlearn societal norms overnight, and perhaps not ever."

"You have a point there," conceded Megan, and wondered, "I guess the only thing we could do is transfer more people from Earth?"

"A bigger selection pool would help," said Veronica, and asked, "But how would we go about it? Should we randomly abduct people, hope we get lucky with a few good ones, and assume that they are heterosexual?"

"The odds would be pretty good that they are heterosexual," said Megan.

"True, but you didn't have children, and neither did I. Not only would they have to be straight, but also willing to make babies. Or do you want to force them to do that?"

"No, of course not!"

"Ok, but if they are not straight, don't want to reproduce, or don't play by our rules, we cannot send them back. But we can't keep them either because we have barely enough resources to sustain ourselves right now. So, we'll just disintegrate them or exile them to the ice age out there?"

"Crap, I don't know. I'm already so stressed about the transfer system and feel guilty because of Walter. I cannot handle much more," said Megan and palmed her face before she asked, "Would the others really vote for something like that?"

"The only reason why we haven't raped and murdered each other is because most of us still instinctively adhere to the conventions of Earth. But sooner or later, they will realize that actions don't have consequences on this planet because we have no laws or police to enforce them. If you give people absolute freedom without limits, most will abuse it in the worst ways. It's only natural, Meg."

"Oh my god, I really want to cry now."

"We could fix it, but remember that it might not be the way it was on Earth," said Veronica, touching Megan's shoulder.

"V, do you really want to sleep with Walter?" asked Megan.

"I've talked to him and watched many hours of surveillance. Walter is brilliant and likes you a lot. But if he weren't dying, I might sleep with him too because he is the only man on this planet that I like."

"It's strange to hear you say that, but do you think he would sleep with you?"

"This is not Earth, and all of us must adapt or perish. But don't worry, I'm not stealing your man, Megan."

"I know, but do you think he would sleep with both of us?"

"I believe so, but he's not the cheating type. Walter would be open and honest about it. Like me, he is not bound by societal norms."

Megan didn't say anything. She stared at the screen of her laptop for a minute, then sighed deeply.

"You are right, I have to digest what you said, but we have to talk about this with the whole colony."

"Of course. Meanwhile, I've ordered your entire shopping list online."

"Thanks, Veronica, that was a big help," said Megan with a smile.

"I got a few items for myself, but I won't make you blush."

"Oh my," said Megan, and giggled a little.

"But I couldn't let them deliver the stuff to my office because I share the building with an investment firm. You'll have to zap a bunch of packages from the porch of my house."

"OK, but I would need to move the relay above your home."

"Is that a problem?"

"No, but I don't have your new address."

"Oh, that's true. You were already here when I moved. Let's do it right now because the first delivery will arrive tomorrow already."

"Yes, let's do that," said Megan before opening her laptop and typing some commands while Veronica observed her attentively.

It took about half an hour for the relay to be in position. Veronica had some junk mail on her porch, and Megan zapped it as a test. A few minutes later, the transmuter spat out a pamphlet from a plumbing company and a business card from a real estate agent. Satisfied with the results, Veronica hugged Megan, left the room, and returned to her quarters.

# 12. Caregivers

After about a month, Lillian refused to bring food to Walter because she no longer wanted to look at the dying old man. Yue took over. She was another perfect female form, and that solidified Walter's perception that this was some kind of supremacy movement. But Yue was scarcely any better than Lillian. Walter made a point to be friendly to her, but that only made things worse. The nicer he was, the more Yue seemed to dislike him.

"Hello, Yue, how are you?" he greeted her with a friendly smile.

"Fine," she mumbled and didn't look at him.

"You did something with your hair, and it looks good," said Walter when he noticed that her hair was in a ponytail.

"Just eat your food," she replied quietly, still avoiding his gaze.

"Oh, what did you bring me today?"

Yue didn't answer. She quickly finished her work and practically ran out of his prison. After a week, she quit the job, and he never saw her again. Yue hated him, or perhaps felt guilty about something, and Walter reminded her of that, which she hated. Walter was sure that Yue was the saboteur: she didn't want Mark here but got Walter by accident, and it weighed on her conscience. Walter wondered if he should tell Megan, but opted to keep that discovery to himself for now.

After Yue stopped, the colony decided to rotate the caretaker duties on a biweekly basis. The next one was Jacques, and Walter disliked the man immediately, but didn't show it. Every day, Jacques entered with some insult or demeaning comment, then laughed at his own callousness. At the end of the second week, he stuck around for a few extra minutes and left the door open. Walter could see that Ahmed was standing right outside of it with a metal rod in his hand.

"You can leave now, old fart."

"I doubt that."

"No, really, just walk out the door. You can go," said Jacques, pointing at the open doorway.

"I'll stay here until your boss tells me otherwise. Get Megan."

"She is not my boss!" yelled Jacques loudly.

"Of course, she is," said Walter, and added, "Now run along. I'm not going anywhere."

Jacques was pissed, walked to the table, and flipped Walter's food tray over. Then, he left the room again, and the door closed behind him.

Irina was the next caretaker. The woman was very professional. She did the work thoroughly and efficiently, but never talked to him at all. She did not even acknowledge anything he said to her. He tried compliments, jokes, vulgarity, and even a few derogatory insults and misogynist slurs, but she showed no reaction whatsoever. Walter was impressed by her discipline and self-control. Irina was not just an astronomer; she had rigorous training.

After Irina, Kevin showed up. Just like when they first met, Kevin was a jerk, but did the job. Walter only spoke to the man on his last day, but he wouldn't have if Kevin hadn't initiated the conversation. Walter was sitting by the table, reading a book, when Kevin picked up the empty food tray.

"You are only alive because Megan sees something in you," said Kevin snidely.

"Something she didn't see you, I guess," replied Walter while continuing to read.

"Shut up!" shouted Kevin and hit Walter in the head with his elbow.

The blow was hard and painful, and Walter dropped the book, almost falling off the chair. He picked up the book from the floor and looked at Kevin unperturbed.

"Oh, did that sting?" asked Walter, raising his eyebrows.

"Times can change. Megan won't always be there to protect you."

"Yeah, but I'll be dead by then, so who cares?" replied Walter, then started to read again and ignored the angry man standing next to him.

Kevin stood there for a moment longer, apparently unsure how to proceed. Walter prepared himself to be beaten again, but then Kevin just stormed out of the room.

Juan seemed to be exempt from caretaker duties, but the doctor visited once every month and was always accompanied by Ahmed. He examined Walter very superficially, taking his vitals and drawing some blood. He asked the same few questions every time, but didn't react to Walter's answers. While he was in the room, he entered some notes on his tablet but showed no concern for Walter's condition and never provided any medication or advice. Ahmed was a brute, and Kevin was a jealous man, but this doctor was on another level. Walter truly disliked him, even more than he had disliked Jacques. But he wasn't entirely sure why; he only sensed that Juan should not be in any kind of caretaker position, not on Earth and not here.

But Sylvie, Megan's niece, was eager to help out. Walter liked Sylvie better than all the others. While they rarely talked to him, Sylvie was chatty and appeared to have a sweet and caring personality. She also bore a strong resemblance to her aunt, with the same hair and eye color, as well as a similar body type.

At first, Sylvie was only supposed to deliver the food, restock the toiletries, and occasionally bring a clean jumpsuit, nothing more. But the girl enjoyed spending hours talking to Walter, and he appreciated her company. They had discussed a great many things, and the conversation flowed naturally. At times, Walter had to remind himself that Sylvie wasn't his friend but still one of his abductors. However, her company kept him sane and mentally active.

"I have known Ron since I was 12, but we were just friends until high school. I studied with him for the exams, but his parents disapproved because I was a girl and Ron wasn't supposed to be alone with me. We sort of dated, but his parents hated that even more because I didn't have the same religion as theirs," said Sylvie, and added, "We didn't have sex, just a chaste kiss once in a while when his parents weren't looking. They insisted that we marry as soon as we turned 18 and were furious when we delayed it until after I graduated from college. They said a woman doesn't need an education. But eventually, they changed their tune when they found out about my condition. They told Ron to ditch me and find a healthy woman instead, one who could pop out a bunch of kids. Ron stuck with me, and I really appreciate that, but I know he was too afraid of his family to ever make a stand. I was astonished that he joined me here. Maybe it's because his friend Juan came along too?"

"That could be, but now you are together and far away from Ron's family," said Walter with a smile.

"That's what I've been telling Ron, but he is still not over it," replied Sylvie, and sighed.

Walter gathered that all was not well in her relationship with Ron. He wondered what issues they might have, but decided not to press her on such private matters.

"Tell me how you got here, Sylvie," said Walter, and changed the topic.

"It's a long story. The story of my life, really. Are you sure you want to hear it?

"Yes, I do. Megan said your illness on Earth was severe. If it's not too personal, I would like to hear about that too."

"The disease started when I was 17, but it wasn't so bad at first. I graduated from high school and was accepted into a reputable university. But by the 4th year, it had progressed so much that I wouldn't see my graduation."

"One day, Aunt Megan told me that she could heal me, but I would have to leave Earth and couldn't return. I knew that Megan was super smart and worked for NASA, but I still thought she had lost her mind. But I asked her what I would have to do. She said that I just have to sit on her patio."

"One weekend, I visited and told her that I would give it a try. She warned me that my life would become very different. But at that point, I was already totally dependent on others and couldn't imagine anything worse than what I was going through. So, I said what the heck, let's do it."

"She helped me out of the wheelchair and sat me down on a blanket on her deck. She said that she would go first, and then she did something on her computer. A moment later, there was a blinding flash, and my aunt was gone. I panicked but couldn't move, so I just sat on the blanket and cried. About 5 minutes later, I passed out without warning. Then I woke up here, and Megan helped me out of the chamber. I was healthy, could walk, and looked so pretty that I didn't even recognize myself. It was the happiest day of my life. Aunt Megan means everything to me."

"That's a wonderful story, Sylvie," he said with a smile and asked, "Were you always close with Megan?"

"No, I never really saw her until I started to get ill, but then she was there for me," replied Sylvie, and added, "I know it breaks her heart to see you like this. I wish she could help you, too."

"It's OK; I'm an old man and have done most of the things I wanted to do in my life."

"You are not that old, and it's not fair! You are nice and have done nothing wrong. You shouldn't have to suffer," said Sylvie, and added more subdued, "I can't believe we voted for this."

"Your friends are letting me die in this way to keep their conscience clear. It's common thinking, and religious people have done that for centuries: instead of being merciful, they are compelled to watch the suffering."

"I know, but we are not some church. I don't know if they are really my friends," said Sylvie, adding quietly, "I'm actually a little scared of them now."

Walter didn't reply, but thought that Sylvie's fears were not unfounded. He got up to use the restroom while Sylvie was cleaning the table. He suddenly felt dizzy while washing his hands and dropped the bar of soap; then he cursed loudly. The soap had fallen behind the toilet bowl and was not easy to retrieve in the cramped quarters for a tall man like him. The alcove for the restroom didn't have a door, just a curtain, and Sylvie rushed inside.

"Are you OK, Water?" she asked, her face filled with concern.

"Yes, I just dropped the soap behind the toilet."

"Oh, let me get that for you."

Walter moved out of the way a little, and Silvie got down on her hands and knees, searching behind the toilet. Walter couldn't help noticing that she had a very shapely rear and prominently displayed it to him. She took quite some time to find the item before she retrieved it. Finally, Sylvie got up again with a huge smile.

"There it is," she said and handed him the bar.

"Thanks, Sylvie, that was very nice of you," he replied and put the soap back on the sink.

"Oh, no problem," replied the young woman and brushed her breasts against him as she exited the restroom through the curtain.

A few minutes later, Sylvie said her goodbyes, and Walter was alone with his thoughts again. Someone unaware or inexperienced might have thought of Sylvie's behavior as innocent, but Walter knew better. This young woman had made her intentions clear. But more importantly, Walter would have to figure out why she was moving in on her aunt's presumed lover. That didn't fit the picture of a grateful niece.

# 13. Spider and Scorpion

Kevin had requested a meeting. He was upset that Megan wasted colony resources on Walter. Megan began to suspect that Kevin was intentionally undermining her authority. Perhaps he wanted to become the leader?

"The prisoner shouldn't be coddled. It defeats the purpose of the punishment," said Ahmed.

"Punishment for what? Most likely, Walter ended up here by accident," replied Megan with a frown.

"Sucks to be him, but that's not our problem," joked Jacques, and several people laughed.

"Painkillers are hard to make with the transmuter, and our supply is limited. Giving them to a dying old man is wasteful," said Juan.

"What kind of doctor are you?" asked Sylvie, and shook her head.

"The pragmatic kind. We have to preserve lifesaving medicine for the colonists."

"We voted to let Walter die on his own. The least we can do is lessen his suffering," insisted Megan.

"I wish he were dead already," said Lillian, and added, "I voted for disintegration. We wouldn't have this discussion if we had done that."

"It's not just the painkillers. You also gave that guy books and glasses, and Sylvie has to spend a lot of time being his nurse," said Kevin.

"Yes, she could be doing useful stuff for the colony," said Yue, and continued, "He is just a stranger. We shouldn't have to cater to him."

"You guys can be assholes if you like, but I will continue being Walter's nurse!" yelled Sylvie, slammed her hand on the table, and left the room.

"Sylvie, wait," said Ron, but she was already out the door.

"Women are too emotional," said Jacques, and he rolled his eyes.

"The problem is that we allowed people to fraternize with the prisoner. Now we have a mess on our hands," added Ahmed, and sighed.

"Megan, you have to make some rules for these meetings. People cannot just leave when they get upset with something," said Kevin, and frowned.

"I will talk to Sylvie later," said Megan.

"How low are we on painkillers, Juan?" asked Irina.

"We have only a few hundred pills. If a colonist is seriously injured, that would not last us very long."

"Can we make more?" asked Ron.

"Yes, but it's a tedious multi-step process, and I don't have the time for that."

"I can help you with that, Juan," suggested Ron.

"You don't know how to do it."

"Can you train me?" asked Ron.

"That takes time, too."

"As you said, we need more painkillers for the colony. Therefore, training Ron would be a good use of your time," said Veronica, and the others seemed to agree with that.

"Fine, I can do that," replied Juan with a frown.

"Walter will die soon, but until he does, we will treat him decently. I will continue to give him two painkillers every day. That's my prerogative as the leader. Meanwhile, Juan will train Ron to make more of them for the colony," said Megan, and concluded, "This meeting is adjourned."

The room cleared out, but Megan remained at the table. She was typing the meeting minutes on her laptop when Veronica approached her.

"How are you doing?"

"Terrible, but thank you for what you said during the meeting."

"Of course, Meg. I will bring the painkillers to Walter tomorrow. I want to check on his mental state while I'm there."

"I was going to ask you to do that. Walter seemed depressed these last few days."

"That's not surprising, considering that he must be in agony. Maybe I can cheer him up a little?"

"Thanks, V."


Walter felt awful today. He spat blood again, and his eyesight appeared to be failing a little more with every passing day. Pretty soon, he would have to ask Megan for stronger glasses, or he wouldn't be able to read the books anymore. Suddenly, the door opened, and Walter expected Sylvie to enter, but it was Veronica instead.

"Hello, Walter!"

"Valkyrie, it's been a while, but I'm sure you have been watching me from afar," said Walter, and asked, "What brings you here today?"

"Megan asked me to check on you," said Veronica, sitting down and crossing her long legs.

"As the interrogator or the therapist?" he asked and got up from the bed to sit with her at the table.

"Maybe a little bit of both," said Veronica, and asked, "How do you feel?"

"A therapist who asks me how I feel - can you be any more cliché?" wondered Walter and added, "I expected better from you."

"Would you prefer our usual dance of spider and scorpion?"

"You being the lovely webslinger, and I the scaly old scorpion? Ominous music playing in the background, the arena lit by only a sliver of moonlight, and the audience on the edge of their seats, wondering which monster will emerge victorious?"

"Precisely, and I love that visual. You have an amazing imagination!" exclaimed Veronica in delight.

"Thanks, let's do that. It might be fun again," said Walter, and nodded.

"Megan and Sylvie swear that you are just a kind old man, but you are not," said Veronica, adding forcefully, "Show me the real Walter!"

"I'll show you mine if you show me yours."

"You might not be able to handle the real me. I can be voracious," Veronica said and smiled sweetly at him.

"And I have a stinger, don't forget that," replied Walter, raising his eyebrows.

"Are you seducing me? Careful, it's working, but… not yet."

"In a different life, that would be fun, too," said Walter, and asked, "But let's skip the banter. Will you tell me what you want?"

"Aww, I was just starting to enjoy myself," said Veronica, and explained, "I came here to cheer you up. Does therapy work for you?"

"Aside from a lot of money, successful therapy depends on several factors: first and foremost, the patient must realize that he has a problem and must have the desire to get better. Then, he must be willing to listen to the advice and follow it. And all of that depends on the persuasion skills of the therapist."

"Do you know that you have a problem and desire to get better, and are you willing to listen to my advice?"

"Persuade me."

"Unfortunately, persuasion doesn't work because you cannot suspend your disbelief. If you even suspect manipulation or dishonesty, you will shut me out. I would have to convince you with facts and logic alone. If you find a flaw in my reasoning, you will mock me and discard my advice. You think of therapy as a battle of wits, and I have to be smarter than you, or the spider will never win."

"True, says the scorpion."

"Some just want a sympathetic ear to voice their misgivings. It's all the therapy they need."

"I'm sure that works for some."

"But not for you?"

"My misgivings are the blank stares that I receive whenever I speak to others."

"Because they don't have the capacity to understand you, let alone relate," said Veronica, and asked, "With 8 billion people on the planet, there must be someone who is your equal?"

"Certainly, I'm not that special. However, the search is exhausting, and all the failures are tiresome."

"I can relate to that. Despite being in a hopeless situation, you are formidable," said Veronica, and asked, "Do you mind my company?"

"I don't mind it, but I prefer solitude."

"Hmm, that's a lie; you do not prefer it," said Veronica and continued, "You are alone because the world disgusts you. You chose solitude because you have given up looking for the one sharp needle in the monumental haystack of ignorance."

"Ouch! Your bite is venomous, but I like the metaphor," replied Walter, and countered, "I gave up and became a hermit, but you gave up too and became merely an observer of whatever flies into your web."

"We are trying to hurt each other, but you love my company, and I love yours," said Veronica softly.

Walter didn't respond, but Veronica's words resonated with him. Just then, he noticed that she had left a couple of painkillers on the table. He nodded to her, then swallowed them with some water, hoping that they would provide a little bit of relief. Veronica watched him without any expression.

"Unlike the others, you have always looked this beautiful, haven't you?" he asked after a moment.

"Would you like to see my picture from Earth?"

"Yes."

Veronica took her tablet and pulled up her picture. It was from her official therapy website, and as Walter had guessed, she looked a bit older but was still a stunning beauty nonetheless.

"The transfer shaved quite a few years off."

"You look lovely, now and then," said Walter with a smile.

"Hmm, that's practically an insult because my appearance is irrelevant to you," replied Veronica.

"Not so. Your appearance has an effect on this old man. Don't sell yourself short."

"Ah, you are reminiscing about your youth," said Veronica.

"Perhaps, but I also appreciate beauty in all things."

"Even a spider?"

"There are some lovely spiders out there. You just have to be careful not to get bitten," said Walter, and Veronica laughed out loud.

For a moment, neither of them talked. Veronica just looked at him intently with her piercing emerald eyes. At first, he held her gaze, but then broke it to drink some water.

"Megan doesn't think you are an old man," said Veronica finally, and asked, "Why do you think she sleeps with you?"

Walter wasn't sure why Megan had slept with him, but it certainly had nothing to do with appearance or affection. He wondered if it would be a mistake to tell Veronica the truth, but then decided to take the risk.

"Keeping me compliant, guilt, pity, loneliness, getting back at her ex, a father complex, or perhaps just boredom or a distraction from work? As a therapist, you are the expert on those things."

"You have listed every possible reason except one. You are selling yourself short," said Veronica, and added softly, "You are still desirable, Walter."

"I doubt that," said Walter, but added with a smile, "but I appreciate the flirtations as much as the next guy."

"You know very well that humans are profoundly irrational, yet you rationalize everything," Veronica said, and then asked, "Do you wonder why I flirt with you?"

"I wonder, but it doesn't matter. It's entertaining and reminds me of my younger days, so don't stop," said Walter.

"Society calls people like us functional. We know how to play the game just well enough not to raise suspicions, but we are still insane."

"Interesting take from a psychologist, but I won't refute that," replied Walter and added with a smile, "Well, Dr. Veronica Parsons, thank you for cheering me up, and I mean that."

"You are welcome, and I mean that too. Someday, we will have more time for our games," said Veronica, then got up and looked around.

"I wish we had windows. I want a big one in my room," Veronica said, but Walter didn't respond to the comment because it seemed like she was just thinking out loud.

"I will still call you Valkyrie. It's a good name for a spider," he said with a smirk.

"An excellent name. Goodbye, my scorpion."

Walter had to admit that Veronica had really put him in a better mood. Her visits were as mysterious as they were stimulating. Of course, not on a sexual level because it was preposterous to believe that a 38-year-old beauty would be interested in a 65-year-old dying man, especially since no money was involved. The flirting was a means to an end, but Walter still hadn't figured out her angle. Sure, he could have pressed her on that issue, but he doubted that she would have revealed her true motives. This spider was extremely cunning.

# 14. Botched Escape

It's been several months now, and Walter's health has been slowly deteriorating, but he was trying to keep in shape with some daily exercise in his small cell. He knew that he would have to make an escape attempt soon before he would become too weak.

His bed broke because a pin that connected the springs to the metal frame had gone missing. Walter had flushed it down the toilet. For two days, Walter had to sleep on the floor, but eventually, Ahmed and Ron came to repair it. Ron carried a toolbox, but Ahmed was armed with a metal rod.

"Hi Walter, I'm Ron."

"Hello, Ron. Sylvie told me about you."

"Just fix the bed, and don't talk to the prisoner," said Ahmed, pointing at the broken furniture.

Walter sat down at the table, and Ron did as he was told. Meanwhile, Ahmed kept an eye on Walter. The repair was slow because Ron didn't have a metal pin, so he had to improvise. Eventually, he moved the bed and flipped it over. Walter peered into the toolbox. He saw several items that could be used as weapons, but a long, sharp screwdriver caught his eye. Ron was moving the bed again, and this time, Ahmed assisted. The heavy metal furniture was not easy to handle, even for two men, so Walter got up and lent a hand. When Ahmed noticed that Walter was standing next to them, he slammed his metal rod into Walter's abdomen. It was painful, and Walter feared he might vomit.

"Stand over there by the wall. Do not approach again!" ordered Ahmed.

Walter complied without protest. He backed up to the wall by the toilet while hiding the screwdriver behind his back. He was armed now and considered killing Ahmed right away by driving the sharp tool into his temple. The big man had bulging muscles, but that made him slow on his feet. More importantly, while Ahmed liked to bully him, he didn't consider Walter a real threat, or he would not turn his back on him.

If the plan worked, Walter would take Ron as a hostage, but would likely have to kill him as well before he made it to freedom. But he knew that Ron was Sylvie's boyfriend, and he liked that young woman. Of course, such sentiments were sorely misplaced: Ron and Sylvie were his captors, just like Ahmed, and their group was letting Walter die a slow death.

The repair was nearly finished, and Ahmed was helping Ron to put the bed upright. While both men were distracted, Walter readied the screwdriver and took a step forward. Just then, the door opened, and Megan entered. Walter hid the weapon and retreated to the wall again. Megan hadn't noticed anything and started talking to Ahmed and Ron.

He silently cursed his bad luck. With three people in the room, he would have to kill both Ahmed and Ron and then take Megan hostage before she could escape. But Megan was his backup plan, and if she fled after he had killed two of her cohorts, she was unlikely to help him. He would starve with two rotting corpses by his side because there was no reason for anyone else to enter this room again until he was dead. The risk was too high, and the odds of success too low. He stashed the tool in the sleeve of his jumpsuit. When the repairs were done, Ahmed, Ron, and Megan left the room again. Walter hid the screwdriver behind one of the bedposts. It was readily available when he needed it, but inconspicuous if his captors found it, because they would assume that Ron and Ahmed had left it there by accident. Hopefully, he would get another opportunity to use it before it was too late for him.


Walter had a chance to escape almost every day because Megan came in the mornings with some painkillers, and Sylvie would spend time with him in the afternoons. She had extended her caretaker duties for another two weeks, and Walter imagined that the rest of the colony was pleased about that. Even Veronica showed up once and, as usual, flirted with him outrageously. Yet Walter didn't take them hostage, and he wasn't even sure why. He was disappointed in himself. He only knew that it wasn't cowardice that prevented him from violence. In fact, he would have enjoyed killing Juan or Jacques. Perhaps Walter had resigned himself to his fate and was too tired to fight for his survival? Or maybe he was foolishly hoping that Megan's audacious story turned out to be true? Was the magnet compelling proof that this was an alien world, or did he suffer from Stockholm syndrome when the victim started to identify with the abusers? Or did he actually care for Megan, Sylvie, and

Veronica, and didn't want to harm them? It was vexing because, for the first time in his life, Walter didn't seem to know himself.

# 15. Sylvie

Megan stopped by again to deliver the painkillers to Walter. She had done that without fail for several months now. Once in a while, she also dropped off a new book, but she never stayed very long and had never slept with Walter again. Most days, she looked haggard, and Walter started to worry.

"Megan, take a break once in a while."

"I can't!"

"If you collapse, the project will be delayed."

"I'm OK, Walter. I can do this."

"I believe in you, Megan. But don't try to save an old man at the expense of your own health."

Megan just nodded, kissed him on the head, and was gone again. Walter admired her tireless dedication. She would sacrifice herself to set right what went wrong, and he almost felt guilty for that, but feared that it wouldn't be enough in the end. His health was deteriorating at an accelerated pace now. Soon, he would not be able to take care of even the most basic necessities.

Megan returned with her laptop later that day. She showed Walter the genetics program of the transfer chamber. It really resembled the character creation process for a video game. Megan loaded Walter's profile, and a few moments later, he stared at himself when he was about 25 years old. It was amazingly accurate, but he noticed that the long scar on his left shoulder was missing. Of course, that made sense since the injury had nothing to do with his DNA.

"OK, that's the base profile. Now we can make some changes to your appearance."

"A fantastic program, Megan!" stated Walter, genuinely impressed with the alien software.

"Go ahead, tell me what you like, and I'll modify it. You will see the result right away."

"Just restore me and make the necessary vicissitudes for my survival on that planet," said Walter, and added, "There is no need for anything else."

"I have already cleaned up your DNA and added the enhancements, but you can look any way you like."

"Megan, my cock is big enough, and if my appearance scares the local wildlife, that's for the better," replied Walter with a grin, and once again, Megan blushed because of the crude expression.

"I agree, you are very handsome," she said and locked in the profile.

Walter was grateful for Megan's work but also concerned. This genetics program was potent, and he was utterly at Megan's mercy. If she wanted to give him horns and a tail, she could do that with a few keystrokes. Assuming that it was all true, nobody should have that much power over the very fabric of life.

A few hours later, Sylvie entered. She brought a new jumpsuit for Walter. He went to the restroom to switch it out, but this time, Sylvie accompanied him. He was feeling pretty well today and was perfectly able to remove it himself, but she insisted on helping him. While doing it, she brushed against his genitals several times. Once he was naked, she offered to wash him in the shower, and Walter agreed because he was curious to see what would happen next. Sylvie adjusted the water flow and temperature, then started applying soap to his body. However, her jumpsuit was getting wet.

"I'll just take this off," she said, then quickly removed her clothing and joined him in the shower cabin.

She soaped his entire body and paid special attention to his groin. Walter couldn't help getting aroused, but she pretended not to notice.

"I'm already wet, so I'll take a shower too," said Sylvie and smiled.

Then she soaped her own skin, especially her perky breasts, until her nipples were hard. She turned around and fiddled with the water again while her butt was pressing firmly against Walter's groin. A moment later, she reached behind and guided him inside her. Sylvie climaxed twice in quick succession and was squealing loudly. Eventually, she turned around again and smiled at him seductively.

"Tell me what you like, Walter. I'll do anything."

"Just do your magic and surprise me," he replied, and Sylvie certainly did.

They had sex for quite a while in the cramped shower cabin and on the bathroom floor. Sylvie was very experienced and keenly aroused. She had no inhibitions, switched it up several times, and did many sexual fetishes that men appreciated. Walter was enjoying it, and Sylvie orgasmed once more before they had finished.

"That was awesome!" she said as they toweled off.

"You are a dirty girl," said Walter approvingly, and she grinned at him broadly.

"You are not going to tell Ron or Megan, right?"

"I won't tattle."

"You are nice, Walter. I wish we could do this all the time, but they are watching this room, and tomorrow is my last day as your nurse."

"Yes, I know. But it was fun, Sylvie."

"My aunt is neglecting you," she said with a frown and added, "But I will do something very special for you tomorrow. You will like it, I promise."

"Oh?" Walter asked, and Sylvie whispered something naughty in his ear before quickly exiting the room.


Walter had to admit that he was enjoying this surprising development. Typically, he wouldn't get involved with women who were in relationships, but as a prisoner, those sensibilities were misplaced. Life was extraordinary: Walter hadn't been with a woman in several years, but in these last few months of captivity, two gorgeous ones had outright demanded his affections, and a third one was intensely flirting with him. Of course, if Megan and Veronica weren't mysterious enough, now he had to figure out Sylvie's motives as well. She had betrayed her boyfriend and her aunt without batting an eye, but why?

Walter pondered the situation for a long time, and he was frustrated that he lacked sufficient information. He considered some pretty wild theories, but in the end, he couldn't find any sensible explanation. This group, cult, colony, or whatever it was, had many secrets, but perhaps that was proof in itself that this place was otherworldly? Nothing like that could or would happen on Earth!

# 16. Megan

In an ironic twist, Ron took care of Walter next. The young man wasn't very chatty, but he was friendly and polite, and he did his job correctly. Walter liked Ron and engaged him in a conversation.

"Sylvie is a nice girl. You are a lucky young man, Ron."

"Thanks. Sylvie is great. She has been my best friend since high school. We will get married someday," said Ron, and his face lit up.

"Wonderful, tell me about yourself."

"Oh, there is not much to tell. I finished school and got a job at a doctor's office. I was doing the billing while Sylvie was in college."

"With Juan?"

"Yes, he hired me. He is a great guy."

"Megan told me that he came here with you. He must be a good friend."

"Yeah," said Ron, but it didn't sound convincing.

"You repaired my bed, and thanks for that. Is that what you usually do around here?" asked Walter, and changed the topic.

"I love doing repairs. It's rewarding work, and there is always something to fix here."

"I liked to do manual labor when I was younger. It's nice to see when a project was finished."

"Yes, it gives me purpose," Ron said, nodding.

"Well, thanks for taking care of me, Ron. It seems that most of you don't like me very much."

"Oh, no problem, Walter. I think they just don't know how to deal with you. It's not a good situation," said Ron, and frowned.

"Yes, maybe that's it," said Walter and concluded, "Well, don't let me keep you from your work."

"OK, I'll be back tomorrow. God bless you, Walter," said Ron, smiled a little, and then left the room.

Walter concluded that Ron had no idea that Sylvie was promiscuous, and his friendship with Juan wasn't what it appeared to be either. He referred to Sylvie as his best friend, not the love of his life, yet seemed to be excited about marrying her, and that was peculiar, too. The young man wasn't stupid but somewhat naïve or unwilling to acknowledge the problems, and so he drowned himself in work.

He had now met all the members of the group. By appearance, they were a bunch of perfect Barbie dolls and bodybuilders or athletes, but only Megan and Veronica had the brains to match their looks. The rest were of average intelligence at best, and none had suitable characters for a colony in outer space. He would die soon, but this settlement had no future either. Why had Megan invited these people to join her here?


It must have been already late that night when Megan stopped by. She didn't bring her laptop and started to undress as soon as the door had closed behind her. Walter was lying in bed, reading a book. Megan took it out of his hands and placed it on the nightstand, then kissed him deeply.

"I don't have much time, but I need it," she said and looked at him thoughtfully.

"Let's see what we can do about that," replied Walter with a smile, and he took his glasses off.

He gently caressed her naked body and kissed her neck. She seemed to like it, but then she stopped him abruptly and shook her head.

"No, let me do it," she said, unzipped his suit, and almost ripped it off his body.

As soon as he was naked, Megan went to work and mounted him. Walter assumed that the surveillance was still active, but she didn't seem to care. When they were intimate the first time, it was gentle and deliberate. But this time, the sex was hard and fast, and Megan was driving it to the point of almost becoming brutal. Walter's weakened constitution could barely handle the onslaught. After only a few minutes, she screamed loudly, climaxed hard, and collapsed on his chest. After she had recovered, she didn't bother to satisfy Walter. Instead, she got out of bed and dressed herself immediately.

"Thanks," was all she said before she ran out of the room again.

If a man could be raped by a woman, this was probably pretty close to that, and it left Walter feeling a little violated. He didn't expect that Megan had that side to her, and it made him reconsider everything he had learned about her so far.

It was also confounding that she left the surveillance active. Maybe she knew that nobody was there, or she did it on purpose because she knew exactly who was watching. Walter considered one last possibility, and it was unsettling: Megan, who claimed that this colony was her life's work, didn't actually care about it because it was just a precursor to her final goal.

# 17. Veronica

A few days later, Veronica took over as the caretaker. Whenever she entered the room, she gave him a bright smile, but Walter noticed that it was an act now. She wasn't that flirtatious anymore, and Walter figured that was because his health had declined significantly. If anything were to happen between them, that time had passed already. Still, they talked often, with witty, carefree banter as their preferred form of communication. But when she thought that he wasn't paying attention to her, she looked quite sad.

"You like them young, don't you?" asked Veronica as she tidied up his room.

Walter wondered if Veronica knew about Sylvie. It wouldn't surprise him if she did. Veronica was keenly aware of everything in her surroundings.

"What can I say? I'm a creepy old man. I'd offer you some candy if I had any."

Veronica chuckled a little, shook her head, and brushed her long red hair back. The motion looked quite natural, but for a second, Walter thought that she had wiped away a tear with the sleeve of her jumpsuit. Was Veronica sad that he was dying?

"Actually, I like mature women and always have, even when I was younger. There is something to be said about a woman who knows what she wants and has a well-developed personality. It's also easier to deal with that because I know what I'm getting myself into," he said.

"Maturity can be very sexy."

"Indeed, and I have not forgotten your true age."

"Me neither. Sometimes, this body feels strange to me."

"It's lovely, Valkyrie," he said, but she didn't react to the compliment.

"What do you do to stop thinking?" she asked suddenly.

"You have asked me that once before," he said and added, "I can't stop thinking, but when it gets too much, I start writing, and it helps."

"I do that too, but not like you, and it doesn't help that much," said Veronica, and it sounded almost desperate.

"Are you alright?" Walter asked, observing her, but she ignored the question.

"Today is my last day here, and I might not see you again, Walter," she said in a neutral voice.

"True, and that's a shame. For what it's worth, you made my imprisonment a little more bearable."

"You made mine more bearable, too," she replied cryptically, then folded his fresh jumpsuit neatly over the back of the chair.

Before she left the room, she extended her hand as if she wanted to shake his. He was hesitant for a moment, but then took it. He felt something in his palm and closed his hand when Veronica withdrew hers. She smiled at him, took the empty food tray, and left the room without another word.

Walter wondered about Veronica's mental state because her question had sounded like a cry for help. She was still one of his captors, but strangely, he was concerned for her. He went to the bathroom to check what she had given him. When he opened his hand, he saw a small vial with about half a dozen painkillers.

"Thank you, little spider," he mumbled to himself and smiled.

Whatever Veronica's agenda, she wasn't as heartless as she presented herself.

# 18. Death?

It's been nearly 6 months since he was captured, and Walter knew that the end was near. Sylvie was his caretaker again, mostly because she had requested that. He had been weakened and in pain for a long time, but in the last two weeks, his health had deteriorated dramatically. He could barely sit up in bed now, and without Sylvie's help, he couldn't make it to the toilet anymore. She spent several hours with him every day and did her best to make him comfortable. But there was always a sexual angle, and often Sylvie's visits felt like abuse, but Walter was too weak to rebuff her advances.

The colony didn't allow Walter to have a razor, so today, Sylvie was trimming his long, itchy beard, and Walter appreciated her care. She was humming a tune while she worked, and Walter listened to it with a thin smile. When she had finished, Walter wanted to lie down again, but Sylvie kept him in the seated position. She got the food bowl from the table and began spoon-feeding him.

"I know it must have been awful to take care of someone in my condition, but thank you."

"It's not awful. Not long ago, I was completely dependent on others for help. I want to take care of you," Sylvie said and whispered longingly in his ear, "I wish we could go to the shower one more time."

"You are a very special person, Sylvie," said Walter, and that made the young woman smile.

"Please eat a little more," she said, and put the spoon to his lips while her other hand was under the blanket, fondling him, but he could barely feel it anymore.

"OK, one more," he said and opened his mouth a tiny bit.

Chewing and swallowing were painful due to the numerous lesions in his mouth and throat. It took a moment, but eventually, he managed to force the pureed food down. Even eating exhausted him now, and he was sure that he wouldn't be alive by the time Megan had finished the new complex.

"Could you get Megan, please?" asked Walter after he had finally managed to get the food down.

"Of course!" said Sylvie and added, "Just relax; I'll get her right away."

Sylvie left immediately, and Megan was out of breath when she arrived only a few minutes later. She sat down on the edge of the bed and touched his cheek with the palm of her hand. Walter opened his eyes, and even that took some effort.

"Megan, these are my final hours," said Walter.

"Please, Walter, it's nearly finished," she whispered.

"The pain is unbearable; I'm almost blind and cannot walk on my own anymore."

"Just a few more days, please!" begged Megan, and her voice started to crack.

Walter slowly reached under his pillow. It took a lot of effort to pull the screwdriver out. He handed it to Megan. She looked at it, puzzled for a moment, but then realized that Walter could have killed her all this time, but hadn't. She stashed the makeshift weapon in her jumpsuit and kissed Walter on the cheek.

"It is not the way I hoped to go out, but know this: I appreciate everything you did for me, and I don't harbor any resentments."

"Walter, no!" sobbed Megan.

"Megan, listen to me carefully because I have one final idea: transfer me right now."

"But it's not finished," cried Megan, and wiped some tears away with the sleeve of her jumpsuit.

"It doesn't matter because it will buy you a little more time. If I'm healthy again, as you say, I can rough it for a while on that new planet."

"It could work, but are you sure? You don't know what you will encounter there," replied Megan, and Walter sensed that there was hope in her voice again.

"It's a risk, but we have no choice. Transfer me now, or let me die."

"I'm going to call a meeting immediately. We will do it," said Megan.

"Thanks, lover," replied Walter with a tiny smile before he closed his eyes again.

Megan looked at the dying man for a moment longer, but then practically ran to the common area and asked Ron to gather everyone. A few minutes later, the whole colony had assembled. Megan took a deep breath and made the announcement:

"Walter has requested to be disintegrated. He doesn't want to be a burden to the colony anymore."

"He lasted longer than expected but will be dead in a few days anyway," said Juan, and shrugged.

"For goodness's sake, it's an act of mercy. He is in excruciating pain!" stated Megan loudly.

"Megan still has feelings for her geriatric lover," said Kevin snidely, and Jacques found that hilarious.

"Shut up, Kevin!" said Sylvie angrily.

"I think we should grant him that request. It's time that he goes," said Irina, and several of the others seemed to agree.

"Yes, let's do it and finally solve this problem," added Ahmed quickly.

"OK, let's take a vote right now," urged Megan.

Although Kevin abstained out of spite, the vote was unanimous, and Megan was deeply relieved. Immediately after the decision was made, she ended the meeting and led Ahmed, Ron, and Sylvie to Walter's room. Walter had dozed off but woke up again when the door opened. Ahmed and Ron picked him up from the bed. He could barely stand straight and feared he might fall if he tried to walk. Sylvie put his left arm around her shoulder, and Megan did the same on the right. Ron led the group out of the room, and Ahmed walked behind them with a metal rod in his hand. They moved very slowly through the corridors. Every so often, Walter felt Ahmed's baton poking into his back. After a few steps, Veronica met them in the corridor, and the procession stopped for a moment.

"You look like shit, Walter."

"Thanks, I take the compliment. If you have anything left to say to me, do it now."

He looked at Veronica, and even with his diminished eyesight, he could tell that she was smiling broadly at him. She looked happy or perhaps relieved, that he was being executed. He was puzzled but couldn't think straight because the pain was excruciating.

"Not yet," said Veronica, and added, "But don't sweat it - you will be in a better place very soon."

"Goodbye, Valkyrie."

"See you on the flip side," was her nonchalant reply as she walked away.

Walter heard Ahmed chuckling, but felt how Megan and Sylvie tensed up at Veronica's final words. Sure, the conversation was morbid, but it didn't match Veronica's body language, and two words stood out again: not yet. But Walter was too exhausted to think about it any further. He needed every ounce of determination to survive until the transfer was made. It seemed like an eternity before they finally reached their destination, and Ahmed and Ron had placed him in the chamber. Megan operated the controls while Sylvie got one last cup of water for him. When everything was ready, Megan closed the lid without another word. Then she initiated the sequence but hesitated to press the final key.

"What are you waiting for? Just zap him already," said Ahmed impatiently.

Megan sighed and hit the button, and Ahmed nodded in approval. Her hesitation to execute Walter probably sold the ruse better. The control lights flashed red, but it took about 15 seconds before the machine started to hum. Then it stopped again, and some blue lights on the console lit up. The whole process took no more than one minute. Megan opened the lid, and Walter was gone without a trace.

Megan left the transfer room in a hurry but noticed that Veronica had been watching from the doorway. She ignored her because her only concern was to get to her quarters and check her laptop. Walter had been near death when they placed him in the chamber. Megan dearly hoped that she had not waited too long. It was crucial for the final phase that Walter reached the new planet and was fully restored.

# 19. Alive!

Walter didn't expect to wake up again and was genuinely surprised that he did. He was even more astonished that he wasn't in pain anymore. The pod was cramped for a tall man like him, so he quickly pushed open the lid of the transfer chamber and looked around. The room was dimly lit, but his eyesight had returned as well. He climbed out of the chamber and immediately felt the higher gravity. It wasn't crushing, but it seemed like he had suddenly gained a bunch of weight.

Walter examined his body. He was young again, naked and very muscular. All his teeth were there, and the lesions in his mouth had disappeared. The itchy beard was gone, and his face was smooth and cleanly shaven. Even the long, ugly scar on his shoulder was no more, and Walter appreciated it. He sat down on the edge of the transfer pod and smiled: it had not been a hoax, and Megan had pulled off a true miracle.

Walter exited the room with the transfer chamber and promptly stumbled over a cardboard box. The transmuter room was adjacent and had been filled to the top with various loose objects and numerous packages, some of which had spilled into the corridor. But aside from the illumination from the controls of the transfer chamber, everything else was dark. Megan had not yet created any lights in the complex, and the building had no windows. It was a serious obstacle because Walter needed to find food and water. Perhaps even more importantly, he had to recover the clone of Megan's laptop. Without it, he wouldn't be able to communicate with her or control anything in the building. But now the item was buried somewhere in that massive pile of packages.

The only solution was to grab something in the dark and drag it to the room with the transfer chamber. Walter must have opened about 50 packages before he got lucky – flashlights that operated with a hand crank. Armed with that, Walter was able to explore the complex. Fortunately, Megan had already connected the water, and the faucets, showers, and toilets were fully functional. Walter relieved himself, quenched his thirst, and then returned to the mountain of deliveries. It would take him days to go through all this stuff to find the laptop.

After a few hours, Walter had gathered the flashlights, nutrition bars, a Bowie knife, several tools, a sleeping bag, and a nice pillow. He was still naked, but the temperature in the building was suitable for that. He laughed out loud when he found a box with vibrators and other pleasure items. He didn't know why they were sent here or who the intended owner was, but instantly imagined that they must belong to Veronica.

"No toys for my little spider," he mumbled to himself and grinned.

The oddest package was a crate of champagne - the good, expensive stuff from France! Walter was tempted to open a bottle and make a toast to Megan, but then decided to put the alcohol away for now. The higher gravity had tired him out. He rolled out the sleeping bag next to the transfer chamber and lay down for a good night's rest. There will be time tomorrow to find the laptop.


Meanwhile, back at the colony, Megan was rechecking the records. Walter's transfer had gone flawlessly, but she wasn't going to trust the data blindly. She had told Walter that he must find the laptop upon his arrival and turn it on so she could communicate with him. But the computer wasn't active, and that worried her. The two most likely explanations were that Walter hadn't found it yet or that the computer wasn't operating correctly. The uncertainty was killing her, but there was nothing she could do about it.

To distract herself, Megan refocused on other matters. Until Walter confirmed his arrival and the condition of the new planet, this colony was still a priority.

# 20. Ugly Sentiments

Two days after Walter's departure, Megan called for a meeting. They had to talk about the colony's future.

"Have we ever found out if Walter was a spy?" asked Ahmed before the meeting had officially started.

"I have talked to Walter on a few occasions, and Megan and Sylvie spent a lot of time with him. He was a tough, disciplined man and did not make a final confession when he died. We have learned very little about him: only his first name, that he writes books, and that he was likely a scientist before he retired. The evidence is meager and inconclusive," reported Veronica.

"What's your best guess, Veronica?" asked Kevin.

"Walter could have been something like a freelancing journalist or an amateur investigator, but most likely, he arrived due to a malfunction in the transfer system."

"We'll remain vigilant, but he's gone, and hopefully, we won't have any glitches again," said Ahmed, looking at Megan.

"I have finally finished the work on the transport system, and it is operational. But Mark has not responded to my recent messages. I hope he is OK," said Megan, and continued with a different topic, "Veronica made a good point the other day: we need to reproduce, or the colony will die out, and we only have two couples right now."

"Kevin and Ron have to get cracking. No more shooting blanks!" quipped Jacques loudly, and that solicited a lot of laughter, but Ron seemed to be uncomfortable with that comment.

"Just match up the single men and women," said Ahmed after a moment.

"Should we draw straws?" asked Yue facetiously.

"Something like that," replied Ahmed.

A lot of commotion and protest ensued! For a few minutes, Megan had to suspend the meeting because the chatter didn't want to die down.

"That's not going to work. We need a bigger selection!" stated Yue forcefully after the room had quieted again.

"But we don't have the resources for that. We could only support a handful of extra bodies—if that," said Megan, and asked, "It took us five years to find 11 people who voluntarily gave up their lives on Earth to come here. Do we know anyone else who would do that?"

"I have a friend who might want to come. He is a good programmer too and could help out if Mark doesn't show up," suggested Irina.

"Ok, that's one. Anyone else know of any potential recruits?" asked Megan, but the room remained silent.

"How can we find more volunteers?" asked Juan, but nobody seemed to have an answer.

"Maybe we don't ask and just take a few people?" suggested Ahmed after a brief pause.

"You want to abduct them?" asked Sylvie, and gasped.

"It's not like we would go to jail for that," said Jacques and chuckled.

"Would they arrive alive and enhanced? Or like that old guy?" asked Yue, looking at Megan.

"Mark's genetic profile was loaded when Walter was transferred. The DNA did not match, and the machine defaulted to a vanilla transfer of the original body. That's why Walter was not enhanced. If we had known that a transfer was in progress, we could have adjusted it on the fly, but not after it was completed," said Megan.

"That's good detective work and easily avoided in the future," said Ahmed.

"I've worked on the transfer system for the last six months. I've calibrated all parts, then checked and rechecked them a dozen times. I've run several tests and even added a couple of safety measures. Everything is as good as it can be, but it's still alien technology, so there are no guarantees," reported Megan.

"Every time you get into a car, there is a risk. I say we try it out," said Ahmed.

"If we abduct random people, they might not want to have children," said Veronica.

"Well, they have to have children," said Ahmed.

"And if they don't?" asked Sylvie.

"Skip the men and just get a few women. Making babies is their purpose, and we'll do the rest," said Jacques quite seriously.

"A breeding program?" asked Veronica, raising her eyebrows.

"Yeah, something like that," said Jacques and nodded.

"It would allow us to raise these kids as good colonists," added Juan, and Kevin liked that idea.

"As long as it's not me, I'm fine with that. I still want a bigger selection, but I can wait until we have the resources for it," said Yue, and it seemed that Irina was in favor of that, too.

"Of course, it would not apply to the original colony members," said Lillian and smiled at Yue reassuringly.

"But it would be a security problem," said Irina.

"The complex is huge and could house a hundred people. We segregate certain areas and keep the women locked up there. Maybe put them to work in some fashion, too," said Ahmed.

"Naturally, we would prefer if they procreate on their own," said Kevin, and added, "but if they don't want kids or don't fit in, they've got to go again."

"How? We can't transport them back to Earth?" asked Megan.

"We do what we did with Walter, and the problem is solved. It would also be a reminder to play nice and maybe even an incentive to make babies," suggested Ahmed, shrugging his shoulders.

"It's a solution," said Veronica in a neutral voice and left the room.

Abduction, imprisonment, segregation, slavery, forced breeding, indoctrination, and even euthanasia - Megan realized then that she had created a fascist utopia for a bunch of savages. It made her frown, but it was a good lesson, too. It would also make it emotionally easier for her to proceed with the next phase.

"I will try to contact Mark tonight and schedule the transfer. We'll resume this discussion when he finally joins us," Megan said, and adjourned the meeting.

Megan went back to her room. She checked her laptop and almost hollered from the excitement. Walter had returned her messages but had written only six words: *battery low, turn on the lights!* Megan realized then that the complex must be pitch black, and the laptop had nowhere to recharge. She hastily scrolled through her notes to figure out how to activate the electricity, but before she could do anything, someone knocked on her door.

"What do you want, V?" asked Megan curtly when she opened it for Veronica.

"It won't take long. Can I come in?"

"Fine, but I'm busy," said Megan, and let Veronica inside.

"There is talk of new leadership for the colony. I thought you should know that."

"What?"

"The colonists believe that you are not strong enough to make the tough decisions. If you hadn't executed Walter, then Kevin or Irina would already be in charge."

"Why tell me? You went along with all their crap and even encouraged it," said Megan sharply and added forcefully, "and what you said to Walter was unbelievably cruel!"

"I liked Walter. It was my way of dealing with the situation. I believe he understood that."

"If that's your way, I really hope you don't 'like' me," replied Megan angrily, but Veronica just looked at her oddly and remained silent.

"Are you serious about the coup?" asked Megan after she had calmed down a little.

"Quite serious, Megan," said Veronica, and asked, "What will you do about it?"

"Nothing," said Megan, and added sharply, "Kevin can lead the colony. Ahmed can disintegrate me, or maybe I just do it myself? I'm done with this place."

"Meg, do you need some company?" asked Veronica softly, putting her hand on Megan's shoulder.

"No, I need to process this on my own," replied Megan and moved away from her.

"OK, I've said what I had to say," replied Veronica with a little smile, and asked, "Before I go, did you ever get my packages from Earth?"

Megan was unprepared for that question. She had totally forgotten that Veronica had ordered a few items for herself. Aside from a handful of token deliveries, everything had been sent to Walter's new planet. Megan fumbled for an explanation while Veronica looked at her expectantly.

"I zapped everything on your porch. If you didn't receive the packages, perhaps they weren't delivered?" lied Megan, but it didn't sound convincing.

"Oh well, I'll just order the stuff again. I will leave you to your work now," said Veronica, then turned around and left Megan's room.

# 21. A New World

Walter finally found the laptop under a mountain of toilet paper. He turned it on and saw Megan's messages, but noticed that the computer was nearly out of power. He quickly messaged her to turn the lights on, but then shut the machine off again to preserve the remaining battery life.

Walter spent the entire day opening and sorting packages. He found a crate that contained physical books, and he loved the selection, which included science, history, philosophy, and classical literature. One book in particular was interesting because it shouldn't have been included, not even by accident. It gave him pause, and he would have to think about this later, but at least he wouldn't be bored for a long time with his eyesight fully restored and so many volumes available. Most of the other items were very useful to a new colony, but some stuff was quite odd, like a box of board games and even a role-playing game. He also found tennis rackets, ping-pong paddles, soccer balls, and basketballs. How was he supposed to play any of that all by himself? Walter assumed that these deliveries were meant for Megan's colony and ended up here accidentally, but that was strange too: were they going to play volleyball on the frozen tundra? He was concerned that someone would notice the material had never arrived. Megan might have to answer some difficult questions.

About eight hours after he had sent the message to Megan, the lights in the complex turned on, making his job much easier. He began to organize the items and relocate them to other rooms. He tackled the kitchen first and stocked it with cutlery, pots, pans, and plates. It was also the only room with an electrical outlet. Walter plugged the laptop in and allowed the batteries to recharge.

Most importantly, the food processor seemed to be operational now, but Walter had no organic material to test it out. He didn't want to sacrifice his meager supply of nutrition bars and military rations, but then he had an idea. He returned to the transmuter room and gathered a variety of cardboard and starch filler materials, then fed them into the machine. After a few minutes, the contraption spat out a few pellets that looked like dog food. Walter hesitated for a moment, then tried a handful, and they were a bit dry but not too bad. He was relieved that his food supply was secure for the moment, considering the mountain of packaging material at his disposal.

After he had eaten, he turned the laptop back on. He went around the complex, took pictures, and then sent them to Megan. A few minutes later, Megan replied with a request for a video call. Walter didn't think that was even possible when he accepted, but then Megan's smiling face appeared on the screen.

"You made it!" she exclaimed happily.

"Yes, and I'm forever grateful, Megan."

"No, I'm forever in your debt for making you suffer so much. I'm so relieved, Walter!"

"Oh, forget that. I'm healthier than I've ever been in the last 40 years and have enough toilet paper to last me a lifetime," joked Walter.

"I saw the pictures of the transmuter room. How many items were there?" wondered Megan.

"Your logs probably have the exact numbers, but there are hundreds of packages and lots more individual items. I haven't even checked all of them yet, but there was some odd stuff that would be useless for a single individual."

"We don't have detailed logs for the transmuter. I've sent a lot of stuff, but not that much," replied Megan, and her voice sounded concerned.

"Then who sent all this?" wondered Walter.

"No idea. It should not be possible for anyone else to do that. The colony has always asked me to get stuff for the group."

"Another saboteur?"

"I don't know, but things are not going well here. I fear that the colony is falling apart."

"Megan, please listen to me: be very careful because your colonists are not who you think they are. Pack your bags, and join me here. You don't owe them anything."

Walter was happy to be alone on this planet and looked forward to a few years of solitude. If Megan joined him, she would not only become his spouse but also his lifetime commitment. Walter liked Megan, but it was a significant risk, considering that they still didn't know each other that well. However, he would never forgive himself if something were to happen to her, and that was the deciding factor when he offered a way out.

Megan was quiet for a while and didn't look at the camera. Walter wasn't sure if she was thinking about his suggestion or just busy with something else. The colony was Megan's baby, but he hoped that she would take his warning seriously. Ultimately, the decision was hers alone, and he would not press any further.

"Thanks, Walter. I will think about it," said Megan finally, and added, "It's very late here, and I have to finish something up. Can we talk again in the morning?"

"Of course, but I have no idea what time it is on this planet since I haven't been outside yet."

"Please go outside and send me some pictures," said Megan with a smile.

"Will do. Let's say we'll talk again in eight hours?" suggested Walter.

"Eight hours is perfect. I will call you then. Goodnight, Walter!" said Megan, smiling broadly at him, and ended the video call.

Walter went back to the pile of packages. He found several boxes with laptops and electronic accessories. The laptops were nearly identical to the one Megan had sent here, but of course, they only had the standard operating systems, not the alien software. Walter was computer-savvy, something he didn't want the colonists to know. While he was sorting more boxes, he duplicated Megan's machine. When it was finished, he checked and found that it had cloned perfectly. He took the clone and hid it under the transfer chamber.

# 22. The Software

Walter decided it was time to take a look at the new planet. The big iris that was the front door opened with a swish, and warm, fresh air flowed into the complex. It was sunny out there, and the star was high up in the sky. But it was more reddish, so it looked as if it were dawn or dusk on Earth. Walter took a few steps outside. The ground under his bare feet was soft and warm. The landscape was covered in lush, green, tree-like plants, and a small, blue lake was nearby. The noises from the wildlife were a strange yet beautiful cacophony, unlike anything Walter had ever heard before. He saw a multi-legged animal grazing on the vegetation not too far away. It was about the size of a pig, and it was not the slightest bit interested in him. Walter sat down on a large rock and enjoyed the natural surroundings. He started up the laptop and sent a few pictures to Megan. It had been over 8 hours now, but Megan had not called him again. He spent about half an hour outdoors, but then decided to go back inside in case the laptop couldn't connect out there. Finally, he received a message from Megan. She was busy with colony matters and couldn't call him today. She would try again in the next few days.

Walter was a little disappointed, but he used the time to build a small shed right outside the entrance area. It was prudent to have another shelter if the complex suddenly reverted to a ball of Play-Doh. He constructed the makeshift building from a few steel struts that he had crafted with the transmuter, along with numerous loose rocks from the surrounding area of the complex. For now, the roof was just a tarp, but he would improve on that when time allowed. Once the structure was standing, Walter moved some essential equipment and supplies to the new shed and stored them in a lockable trunk.

Walter returned inside the complex and studied the alien software on the cloned computer to avoid interfering with Megan's work on the original one. It was very complicated, almost overwhelming, but the cloned computer had all of Megan's notes, too. That was immensely helpful because Walter didn't have to start from scratch. Megan's research was a rigorous trial-and-error process, but Walter attempted a different approach when he noticed that the software was actually intuitive, just not for humans. Soon, Walter recognized a few patterns and struck gold: the software was able to transform the interface into a more human-friendly one. Instead of pages of alien characters that he couldn't read, it displayed color-coded buttons and links now. He was fascinated by the system and promised himself to learn everything he could about it.

One of the first things Walter checked out was the remarkable genetics program for the transfer chamber. He found that the alien contraption had other powerful features that Megan had never discovered. He also realized that Megan had stored everyone's DNA profile, both the modified and the vanilla versions. He studied them and found a few interesting surprises and unusual, alarming discrepancies.

That piqued his interest further, and he then learned about the relays. It took him a while to find the one in Earth's orbit and even longer to figure out how it could access the internet. But once he succeeded, it opened many doors because the relay could bypass logins, passwords, and even the toughest encryptions. He conducted searches on Megan and the other colonists, digging deeper by investigating emails, text messages, social media, public records, and even bank accounts – if he could find it, the relay could hack it. Next, he pinged the relay above the colony and discovered that it had stored useful information as well, including connections, operating times, user logs, and surveillance footage, and not just of his prison cell.

Furthermore, Megan recorded all colony meetings and amended the footage with the minutes she took. Water studied all the new information in detail, and after only a few hours of intense detective work, a much clearer picture of the colony and its people emerged, forcing him to reconsider quite a few things. Walter had focused on the improbable story of extraterrestrial colonies, but that turned out to be true. The real deception, as it often was, lay with the humans, and he scolded himself for being blind to the obvious.

The more Walter explored the alien program, the easier it became to understand. It was almost as if the software had begun to anticipate what he wanted to do. He suspected that it was actually some kind of AI, and he had found a way to communicate with it. Next, Walter explored the building plans. He had been right about the waste disposal reservoir, and the transmuter and transfer chamber were drawing resources from that. But it didn't stop there. The big ball was actually resting on an underground stem that extended deep into the soil. It had countless tendrils or roots that spread out in a wide radius. The aliens were mining the planet, and that's how the machinery was supplied. Deep within the stem was the power source, but Walter couldn't figure out what it actually was. He suspected that it must be nuclear fusion or something even more powerful.

Once he got a handle on the building process, he made some subtle changes to his complex – more lights, more electrical outlets, door locks that worked a little differently, and even a room with a window, although he would have to make the glass pane separately with the transmuter and install it by hand because the aliens didn't know about windows. However, he took great care not to interfere with Megan's work, as he didn't want to reveal that he now possessed that capability. The alien system was incredibly potent, and by the end of the day, Walter was already far ahead of Megan's understanding.

# 23. Exodus

Megan checked her laptop one last time before she went to bed. Walter hadn't responded to her messages in several days. Megan resolved that it was time to transfer to the new planet without further delay, but she couldn't leave Sylvie behind. Sylvie was still awake, playing cards with Yue in the common area. Megan asked her to come to her room when they had finished. Sylvie arrived only a few minutes later.

"Can I trust you, Sylvie?" asked Megan as soon as the young woman entered.

"You are my aunt and saved my life. Without you, I would be worse off than Walter was or even dead by now," said Sylvie, and added forcefully, "Of course, you can trust me!"

"Walter is not dead."

"What do you mean?"

"Walter is healthy and on another planet."

"Wow, that's fantastic news! I'm so happy! How did you do that?" exclaimed Sylvie, bouncing on her toes and clapping her hands.

"Instead of killing him, I transferred him there. He is enhanced now and has a place to live, but is all alone," said Megan, and added, "I want to join him and would like you to come with me."

"Yes! When are we leaving?"

"Are you sure?"

"I don't like these people anymore."

"Me neither, and that's why I want to go," said Megan, adding, "We will leave tonight. You can bring Ron, of course, but we won't bring anyone else."

"OK," said Sylvie, but she seemed to be undecided.

"Is everything alright between you two?"

"I'll talk to Ron," she replied, adding, "I'll be back in a few minutes."

As soon as Sylvie left the room, Megan prepared the transfer protocol. Sylvie and Ron had no experience with the chamber, so Megan automated the three transfers. They could be executed in quick succession without the need to use the controls of the alien machine. She had already finished the code when her niece finally returned. Sylvie looked annoyed.

"Is something wrong, Sylvie?"

"No, it's OK. Ron was being difficult again. He wanted us to bring Juan as well. I told him that's not going to happen. He got upset about that, and we argued, but he is coming and will meet us in the transfer room."

"OK, I have automated everything, but I have to go first because Walter has no experience with the alien technology," said Megan, and hesitated for a moment before she added forcefully, "I want you to come right after me, Sylvie!"

"Of course, Auntie. Let's meet Ron at the machine. He should be there by now."

"Yes, let's go."

Ron was already waiting in the dimly lit room. He looked nervous but was happy to see Megan and Sylvie. Megan explained the procedure to him and her niece:

"Sylvie, after I've transferred, you have to wait until the lights go blue. Then, open the lid, press the key on the controls, enter the chamber, and close the lid. That's all you have to do," said Megan, addressing Ron: "The machine will hum, and the lights will go red for about 30 seconds. Then the chamber stops, and the lights go blue. You open the lid, press the key, get inside, and close up again, exactly the same way as before."

"Got it," said Ron, and Sylvie nodded.

"Alright, I see you guys on the new planet," said Megan, and hugged both Ron and Sylvie.

Then she pressed the button on the console of the machine, entered the chamber, and closed it. A few seconds later, Megan lost consciousness, and the transfer had begun.

# 24. Arrival

Three days ago, Megan had messaged him, asking how he was doing. Walter replied that he was a little tired and suspected that the higher gravity was taking its toll on him. The next day, Megan messaged again, but Walter didn't reply. The following day, he ignored her message once more and allowed the computer to run out of battery.

The day after that, the transfer chamber was activated. Just before the six hours were up, Walter placed the discharged laptop on the console of the machine, then laid down in front of it and was perfectly still. The transfer finished, and a few minutes later, Megan exited the chamber. She saw Walter lying motionless on the floor and noticed the laptop by the controls. She checked it out and tried to start it again, but without power, it didn't work. The transfer chamber closed up and began to hum again. Megan glanced at the controls and seemed satisfied. She took the laptop, stepped over Walter's body, and was about to leave the room when Walter pretended to wake up.

"Megan!" he shouted, standing up.

Megan screamed a little, turned around, and looked like she had seen a ghost.

"Sorry, I was waiting for the transfer to finish, but I must have dozed off."

"Walter, I didn't see you there. Are you feeling alright?" she stammered.

"Oh yes! But I have messed up the laptop. It's not working anymore."

"It's probably just out of charge. Did you not get my messages?"

"No, I couldn't get the laptop to work again. I'm not that good with computers."

"Oh…" mumbled Megan, still staring at him as if he were an aberration.

"That was fast, Megan. I didn't think you would come so soon," said Walter, and embraced her.

"My goodness, you look awesome!" she said, hugged him back, and Walter could tell that Megan had finally gained control over herself again.

"I look and feel like I did when I was 25. Thanks for that, Megan," replied Walter with a smile.

"I had to get away from that place and from those people. Sylvie and Ron are coming too. I hope you are not mad that we are disrupting your solitude so soon?"

"Of course not, and I completely understand. Besides, you and I still have some catching up to do, if you know what I mean?" asked Walter, but Megan blushed furiously and turned away from him.

"Are you alright?" asked Walter.

"I didn't mind getting naked in front of you, not even the first time, and I don't mind being naked right now. I had several boyfriends and was married, as you know. I'm not shy, but I have a weird inhibition about talking about intimacy. But I promised myself to be more open-minded," said Megan, then faced him again, and added, "Yes, we should have sex, and I'm looking forward to it. There, I said it."

"That's the spirit!"

"Next time, I will try to say it a little sleazier," said Megan and winked at him.

"I can't wait to hear you talk dirty," replied Walter, and put his arm around her shoulders.

"Watch out, I'll make your ears burn….in about 10 years!" she said and laughed out loud.

"Sylvie won't be here for a while," said Walter, pointing at the humming machinery.

"Yes, it will take six hours for the transfer to be completed," said Megan, blushing and adding, "Do you want to be with me?"

"That's so tempting, Megan," he said and laughed before adding, "but you just got here; let's get you settled in first. We'll have plenty of time for the sweet stuff later."

Megan readily agreed and seemed relieved. Walter gave her a quick tour of the complex and even took her outside. Megan was satisfied with the building and loved the new, warm planet. They returned to the transmuter room.

Walter had already cleaned up much of it, but there was still some work left to be done, and Megan was eager to help.

"Walter, how long did you have that screwdriver?" she asked after a while.

"For several months. I got it when Ahmed and Ron repaired the bed that I had sabotaged."

"Why didn't you use it?"

"Ahmed was as good as dead, but you walked into the room in the nick of time."

"Maybe I should have been a little slower?" wondered Megan with a frown.

"If you didn't enter when you did, we would not be here today."

"I don't understand?"

"I would have killed Ahmed and taken Ron hostage to force my way out of that room, only to realize that there was no escape because your story was true," said Walter, and concluded, "but at that point, you wouldn't have helped me any longer. Then, I would have to kill all the other colonists or be killed by them. Even if I had survived that, I would have still died of the radiation in the end. Ironically, by inadvertently saving Ahmed's life, you saved mine, too, and we ended up together in a better place."

"You called Veronica a psychopath, but she once warned me that you were like her. Are you a psychopath?"

"I'm not sure if I'm a psychopath, but I have a few things in common with Veronica."

"Could you have killed everyone?"

"I would have killed them out of necessity, not for enjoyment. Except Jacques - I think I would have appreciated his demise. Maybe castrate him before I put him out of his misery. Oh, and I wouldn't have killed your doctor," replied Walter very casually, and he could tell it had an effect on Megan.

"Juan? Why?" she asked carefully.

"Juan would have begged for death, only to be denied," said Walter, and added calmly, "I have my reasons."

105

Walter's chilling words triggered the desired result. He saw that all color had drained from Megan's face. She must have finally realized that Walter wasn't some random old guy but a dangerous man. She probably wondered if he had noticed that she thought he was dead when she arrived. If he were aware of that, Megan might face a gruesome reckoning here.

"You were angry because the colony treated you horribly. You suffered so much," Megan said after a moment and kissed his cheek, but Walter didn't react to that.

"I told you once that you don't know someone until you see how they react in an extreme situation."

"I remember that."

"I found out that I did not know myself."

"Do you regret it?"

"It disturbed me, but I don't regret it. You, Sylvie, Ron, and even Veronica should live."

"Veronica? She was so callous. What she said before the transfer was heartless, and I will never forgive her for that. She deserves to die!" stated Megan forcefully, and her words confirmed what he already suspected.

While Walter was sorting packages, he noticed that Megan spent a lot of time with the controls of the transfer chamber. She told Walter that she wanted to check if everything was alright, but he knew that she was trying to program the machine for a quick return home. After a few failed attempts, she looked frustrated and worried. Walter used the restroom, checked the cloned laptop, and was surprised to discover that the old colony no longer existed. When he returned to the transfer chamber, Megan was quietly crying while desperately punching commands into the machine. He pretended not to notice and continued sorting through the deliveries.

Six hours later, Megan was still working on the controls. All lights were turning blue, and she seemed satisfied with the readings. She nodded to Walter, and he opened the lid of the chamber. Sylvie was just waking up with a big yawn.

"Hi there, sleepyhead," quipped Walter.

"Walter! You look so healthy and handsome!" exclaimed Sylvie happily and jumped out of the pod.

"Thanks, Sylvie. Without your tireless care, I would have never made it here."

"Think nothing of it. You know I loved taking care of you and will do it again," said Sylvie, and hugged him fiercely as her hand brushed against his genitals ever so slightly.

"Thanks, girl. I appreciate that. But now it's my turn to take care of you on this new world," said Walter and handed her some water.

"The machine has initiated again. Ron must be on his way. We have another 6 hours before he is here," said Megan, smiling at her niece, but Sylvie suddenly looked very apprehensive.

"Good, Meg and I made some real food, and we even have an alcoholic beverage for a toast. Let's go to the kitchen," said Walter, and put his arms around Sylvie and Megan.

After they had eaten and shown Sylvie the new colony, all three of them continued to organize the complex. Walter was moving his bed and possessions from the room with the transfer chamber to empty quarters down the hall. Megan continued to work on the controls, and Walter could tell that she was thoroughly frustrated. With the cloned laptop, he checked on her progress and ensured that she couldn't do any harm.

Meanwhile, Sylvie helped him with all the books. As usual, Sylvie was chatty, and they talked a lot about the new planet. It was just a casual, friendly conversation, but when they were alone in the empty room, Sylvie's demeanor changed.

"Walter, did you change a lot about your looks?"

"No, this is what I looked like when I was your age."

"Megan didn't modify anything?"

"Well, the long scar on my left shoulder is gone," said Walter, pointing at his upper arm.

Sylvie put some books down and came closer to him. She traced with her finger roughly where the scar had been on his skin. Of course, Walter knew exactly what she was doing.

"I think that scar made you even hotter. I liked it when we were in the shower," said Sylvie, and added, "You must have been very popular."

"I did a few crazy things when I was young."

"I know you are experienced," said Sylvie, and asked, "I'm so glad Megan saved you. You must be very grateful to her?"

"I'm happy to be alive and out of that prison," replied Walter truthfully.

"Walter, will you do crazy things with me?" asked Sylvie and embraced him.

"Your aunt and boyfriend might not like that."

"Oh, they don't have to know. It will be our little secret," Sylvie said seductively and pressed herself harder against his body.

"We'll see what the future holds," he replied, gently brushing a strain of her blonde hair away from her eyes, but then let go of the embrace.

Sylvie bit her lip in a cutesy way and smiled at him broadly. He smiled back at her and continued to organize the room.

# 25. Revelations

Six hours later, Megan, Walter, and Sylvie returned to the transfer chamber. Sylvie looked unhappy, but Megan assured her that the transfer was going fine after she had checked the readout from the machine. A moment later, the lights were turning blue, and a few minutes after that, Megan opened the lid.

"V?" mumbled Megan in surprise when she saw who was in the pod.

"Did you expect someone else?" Veronica asked with a yawn as she woke up.

"Frankly, we did," said Walter, looking expectantly at the redhead inside the pod.

He wasn't surprised that Veronica showed up here. In fact, 'not yet' made a lot of sense now. She hadn't been cruel when she spoke to him before his execution because she already knew what would happen and knew that they would meet again on this planet. The real question was how Veronica had discovered the plan when Megan and Walter had been so careful about it.

"Wow, you look studly now, but a tad too young for my taste," said Veronica, and checked out Walter's physique unabashedly.

"Thanks, but I'm still an old fart at heart," replied Walter with a thin smile.

"Hmm, I'll have to remind myself of that," said Veronica, and climbed out of the chamber.

"So, what are you doing here?" asked Walter.

"Oh, you always knew that I would come. I'm your needle, and you are mine."

Megan and Sylvie were confused by that comment, but Walter remembered her words: the one sharp needle in the monumental haystack of ignorance. No doubt, she was a sharp needle, but he was not so sure if she was the one he was looking for, and more importantly, she was certainly not here for him.

"Veronica, where is Ron?" implored Sylvie.

"He didn't make it," replied Veronica simply, and Sylvie stared at the redhead in disbelief.

"You killed my boyfriend to take his place! You bitch!" shouted Sylvie.

For a second, Walter thought he had to intervene to prevent a fight. He doubted that Veronica had disposed of the young man to get here. It was simply not her style.

"I didn't kill anybody, or at least not Ron. Ahmed and Juan killed him on Kevin's orders, and Irina is dead too."

"What? I don't believe you!" yelled Sylvie, but Veronica was unfazed.

"I recorded the whole thing and sent it here before I transferred," replied the redhead calmly.

Megan used the laptop to retrieve Veronica's files. They gathered around the computer and watched the video recordings together. The first file was about 7 hours old. Kevin and Irina had a big argument in the common area. It wasn't clear what caused the shouting match, but eventually, Kevin slapped Irina across the face, and matters quickly escalated after that. Irina had some serious fighting skills and was winning the brawl against the larger, stronger man. But Ahmed suddenly put the woman in a chokehold from behind. Irina fought to get free, but Ahmed threw her on the ground and then kneeled on her throat while Jacques was holding down her legs. Irina struggled for a while longer until her body suddenly went limp.

The second file was recorded in the last hour before Veronica transferred, and the footage was even more harrowing: the camera showed the transfer chamber, and the lid was closed. Kevin, Ahmed, and Juan rushed into the room, trying to stop it. Ron interfered and argued with Kevin and Juan until Kevin told Ahmed to step in. Ahmed beat Ron with the metal bar, and the young man went down. Then, Juan proceeded to stomp on Ron for several minutes until he stopped moving. All the while, Lillian, Yue, and Jacques were watching the show from the doorway.

Kevin couldn't stop the transfer. He gestured wildly, then slammed his fist on the controls of the machine. Lillian came to comfort him, but he rudely brushed her off. Meanwhile, Juan was crying in the corner of the room, perhaps regretting Ron's murder. Eventually, Ahmed and Jacques dragged the lifeless body from the room, leaving a trail of smeared blood on the floor. Kevin and the rest of the people followed, but Juan remained, still crying. A few moments later, Ahmed came back, picked Juan off the floor, and yelled at him. Eventually, Juan nodded, and both men left the view of the camera. A minute later, Veronica appeared, activated the transfer chamber, and got inside. She quickly typed something on her tablet, then shut the lid of the chamber. The recording ended with the transfer room seemingly warping and distorting until the camera went black.

Sylvie was crying, and Megan tried her best to calm her niece down. But surprisingly, after only a few minutes, Sylvie had composed herself again.

"I'm alright," was all she said, and nodded a little.

"Veronica, that's disturbing footage. Please tell us everything from the start," said Walter.

"The short version first, because I need to get it off my chest: you didn't do your homework, Megan!" stated Veronica and wagged her finger a little.

"I know that now, but what's the explanation for all this?" asked Megan, and sighed.

"Just after you had transferred, someone must have told Juan about it, or maybe Ahmed saw it on the surveillance. Juan and Ahmed woke everyone up and brought them to the common area. When most of us had gathered, Kevin made a long, angry speech claiming you had abandoned them and then declared himself the leader. However, Irina insisted that we vote on it. Kevin dismissed it and then called Irina a traitor and a spy. That's how the fight started."

Walter was reasonably sure he knew who had informed Juan about the transfer. But that had to wait for now.

"After they killed Irina, Juan realized that Ron and Sylvie were missing. That's when they all rushed to the transfer room, but Sylvie was already in the chamber. Ron begged them to let her go, but Kevin was adamant about stopping the process. Ron blocked access to the controls, and that enraged Kevin so much that he told Ahmed to 'fuck that little faggot up'. Ahmed did,

111

and Juan protested at first, but then attacked Ron while he was down. Well, and you saw the rest."

"Nobody helped Ron?" asked Megan.

"No, Lillian and Yue just watched, and Jacques was laughing the whole time."

"Fucking bastards!" shouted Sylvie.

"Please continue, Veronica," said Walter.

"Lillian hated that her husband was your ex and even more that he had to defer to your leadership. She incited Kevin to take over so she could be the queen. Kevin still thought of you as his property and never forgave you for prioritizing your dreams over him. Ahmed was a sadist who was dishonorably discharged for assaulting a superior. His penchant for safety and security was merely an excuse to harm someone, and he ultimately got his wish. I learned during our sessions that Yue was a vindictive woman out for revenge, but more on that later."

"Our astronomer slash martial arts expert was selling us out to someone back on Earth. I never figured out who that was – possibly a government agency or a corporation – but I caught Irina using the relay to send coded messages to someone. Jaques was a perv, one of those Andrew Tate fans. He had several restraining orders against him. He joined only because Lillian let him believe that he could fuck a bunch of pretty girls. Juan was ashamed that he was gay since that didn't mesh well with the Latin machismo. He also had less compassion than I have, which is particularly concerning, considering he was a doctor. He didn't cry for Ron; he cried for himself."

"I had no idea," whispered Megan and palmed her face for a moment before she said, "but Juan was Ron's friend. I don't know much about him, but they always seemed close."

"They were very close, knew each other for years, and then Juan just killed him," said Sylvie with a sniffle, and Megan put her arm around her again.

"It's good that Mark never came because he shouldn't have been there either. He had a long and shady history. He was fired from his job last year because he had a drug and gambling problem and used company money for his vices.

More recently, he was indicted on charges of fraud as well. I believe the threat of prison time was the real reason why he finally agreed to join us."

Walter watched Megan's reaction closely. She seemed angry and disagreed with Veronica, but did her best to hide it.

"Your colonists were assholes, and they were plotting to overthrow you," concluded Veronica with a sigh.

"How do you know all this?" asked Walter.

"I was going to be stuck with a dozen strangers on another planet, so I did due diligence on them. Additionally, I'm skilled at reading people and getting them to open up to me. That's part of my job."

"It's hard to believe that we ended up with so many bad apples," said Sylvie, shaking her head.

"Maybe the colony turned them into bad apples?" wondered Megan before she asked, "V, why did you still join us if you knew all this?"

"Oh, it's nothing I couldn't handle. Maybe I joined because I'm a bad apple, too?"

Nobody responded to that remark, but Walter smirked a little because both Megan and Veronica knew why she had joined, and this exchange was just for his benefit, and maybe Sylvie's, too.

"What else do you know?" asked Walter after a moment.

"Lots of things," said Veronica, but suddenly changed the topic and asked, "Is nude our new dress code?"

"We just arrived here, and there was no time to make clothes yet. But this planet is pleasantly warm, so we'll be fine in the buff for a few days," said Walter, and asked humorously, "You aren't shy, are you?"

"No, but if I look at your equipment all the time, I might get ideas," replied Veronica and continued, "But back to the story: Yue hated Mark ever since he got her pregnant a few years ago and then bailed on her without warning. She wanted him to die during the transfer, but she messed up and transferred Walter instead. She knew that Kevin was jealous of Mark, so Yue sweet-talked Kevin into helping her clean up the logs; it also involved a blowjob that Lillian didn't know about."

"I didn't need to know that part either," muttered Megan, slightly embarrassed, but then said sternly, "Your vote was the deciding one when we discussed Walter's fate. You condemned him to a terrible death so you could study him for longer!"

"Oh, please, Megan! I knew you would try everything you could to save Walter because that's your nature. The colony voted overwhelmingly for Walter's demise, and my vote wouldn't have mattered. But if I had voted for immediate termination, you wouldn't have had the time to develop a plan. So, I went with the slow, painful death, and that also gave me time to make my own arrangements."

"You didn't want Walter to suffer and die?" asked Megan.

"I joined because I was bored out of my mind on Earth – day in and day out, I had to deal with depression, anxiety, phobias, and marital problems, blah, blah, blah. I thought a new planet with a select few people would be fun, but it wasn't as entertaining as I hoped. Sure, they were all messed up, but in pretty mundane ways. Then Walter arrived, and oh my, I was almost in love with him because he's as crazy as I am, but hides it a little better. Of course, I didn't want Walter to die!"

"I think you have me beat on the crazy, but it's nice to know that you wanted me to live," said Walter.

"I suspected that Megan wasn't actually sleeping with you but secretly discussing her plans. The surveillance was off, so Valkyrie - I love that name - placed a listening device in the room, and I was always up-to-date," said Veronica.

"You knew everything!" exclaimed Megan, and she seemed genuinely shocked by that revelation.

"I did, and you taught me what I needed to know about the new planet and the alien controls," admitted Veronica.

"Why didn't you tell me? Why did you pretend not to care?"

"The colony was your life's work. When I arrived, you were so happy there, almost euphoric. You couldn't see the warning signs, and I don't think you would have listened. So, I watched over you but let you find out the hard way."

"Tough love," said Walter, nodding.

"Tough love," repeated Veronica earnestly, but then playfully returned to her previous remark, "Well, one time you did have sex, and I was so jealous. Judging by the grunts and moans, it must have been terrific?"

Veronica grinned provocatively at them. It looked as if Megan would die from embarrassment, but Walter just put his arm around her shoulders and chuckled a little.

"It was excellent, and thanks for asking," said Walter, and then changed the topic, "You must have sent all those packages here?"

Walter was surprised that Veronica didn't mention the second time when they were intimate. With Megan screaming so loudly, she surely must have heard it on the recordings.

"Nice, but now I'm jealous again," said Veronica and answered, "Of course, I've sent them here. Your idea about ordering online was ingenious, and Megan inadvertently showed me how to retrieve stuff from my porch. I'm not your typical woman, and shopping bores me, but I wanted this place to be well-stocked when you arrive here. Do we have the champagne?"

"We do, but you went overboard. I was drowning in packages!" stated Walter and laughed.

"Oops!" replied Veronica and changed the topic, "You were correct that I'm a psychopath. But I like to think of myself as the good kind of psycho. You don't have to watch your back around me. I don't cut people up and eat them, and kill only when it's necessary."

"That's so reassuring, V," said Megan sarcastically, and that made the redhead giggle.

"Meg, I'm on your side. Not just because you paid me a small fortune in therapy fees, but because I like you. You are a good person, and I admire that, even if I cannot be like you," said Veronica, and added, "I know Walter doesn't mind, but you and Sylvie are freaked out to have me here – don't be, just give me a chance. You might need a psycho someday."

"What happened to the others?" asked Megan a moment later.

"Oh, they are all dead or will be pretty soon. Thanks to you, I knew how to reverse the building before I left. By now, it should just be a big ball of Play-Doh again. If they weren't pancaked, they are popsicles outdoors, and it serves them right!"

Walter was not surprised by Veronica's admission of multiple murders. He had long suspected that she was capable of such deeds, but in this case, he couldn't fault her for it. Meanwhile, Megan turned so pale that Walter thought she might faint, but it wasn't the mass killing that shocked her. He had a good idea why Megan was so distraught, but it was not the time to reveal the truth yet.

"I agree with you there, Veronica," said Walter, nodding.

"We are monsters. I knew you would approve," said Veronica, and Walter understood the reference while Sylvie looked puzzled again, and Megan just frowned.

"You are scary, but I don't hate you. I was mad because I thought you did something to Ron," said Sylvie and smiled a tiny bit before she added, "I'm glad you killed those bastards, Veronica."

"Ron was a good kid. We talked often about the issues with his parents. He didn't deserve this," said Veronica, and Walter silently agreed with her.

"Walter, this is your planet. What do you say?" asked Megan, and Walter nodded.

"I'll be watching you," he said sternly, but gave Veronica a little smile.

"Oh, please do!" replied Veronica in a sultry voice, then laughed happily and asked, "And that brings up an interesting point: Meg, do you remember our talk about how things have to be a little different from Earth?"

"I know, I know. But can this wait for now?" asked Megan, once again looking very uncomfortable.

"We have three chicks and Walter. It's best to clear the air right away."

"What does she mean?" Sylvie asked, looking at her aunt, and Megan blushed furiously.

"Veronica wants us to share Walter," she said, sighing.

"Share Walter? You mean we all sleep with him?" asked Sylvie with a look of utter shock on her face.

"Yes, and she is right."

"I don't do that; I'm not a slut!" insisted Sylvie and shook her head.

"You loved Ron, yet you shared him for years," said Veronica.

"What?"

"Ron was gay, and Juan was his lover."

"Juan? The guy who killed him? You are lying. Ron has slept with me!" protested Sylvie loudly.

"Search your heart, and you'll know the truth."

It seemed like Sylvie wanted to protest, but remained quiet for a moment before she said:

"But why would Juan kill Ron if that's true?"

"It's complicated, Sylvie. Juan wanted Ron, but at the same time, hated himself for that. He was ashamed to be gay. Ron was his desire, but also symbolized the disgrace. Juan killed Ron because he irrationally believed that it might make the shame go away. It didn't, and he cried over that."

"That's so fucked up!" said Sylvie and sat down on the floor.

Veronica had given a plausible explanation, and Walter was curious how Sylvie would handle the news. She seemed depressed at first, but then stood up again, nodded, and returned to the previous topic.

117

"We are bartering over Walter as if he were a piece of meat. That's not fair to him."

"You are right. It is unfair. Walter, what do you say?" asked Megan.

"This tiny colony cannot survive without new ways of thinking," said Walter.

"Could you sleep with all three of us?" wondered Sylvie.

"In time, I believe I could."

"But?" asked Veronica, raising her eyebrows.

"Not yet," said Walter, looking at her expectantly, and Veronica's reaction was priceless: for a moment, she just stood there with her mouth agape.

"Touché, my scorpion," she said softly and then kissed Walter on the cheek.

"We have to come to terms with the tragedy, and especially Sylvie needs time to adjust."

"That's an understatement," mumbled Sylvie, but Walter noticed the tiniest smile on her lips.

"When all of us are ready, we will work out the details," said Walter, adding with a smirk, "Luckily, you are covered until then since your special delivery has arrived undamaged, Veronica."

"Nice, but that's just the consolation prize," said Veronica with a slight pout.

Veronica appeared to be a little disappointed by the delay, but Megan nodded ever so slightly, and Sylvie frowned but didn't object. Walter wasn't surprised and smiled a little. For a while, nobody said a word until Veronica spoke again.

"I won't tell you the whole story, but Walter gave me a new name when we first met. It started as a joke, but I realized that it had a much deeper meaning. Please call me Valkyrie from now on. A new planet deserves a fresh start."

"It's a pretty name," said Sylvie quietly.

"Alright, Valkyrie," said Walter and quipped, "What the heck, maybe I'll change my name too if I can think of a good one?"

"With Ron gone, the old me is gone too. I want a new name," said Sylvie firmly.

Megan was surprised but smiled fondly at her niece. It seemed that she was thinking of a new name for a moment before she spoke:

"Do you like Nadya?"

"Oh, that's a pretty name, too," said Sylvie and nodded.

"We should shed our old skins like snakes do. It will be fun, and maybe we can even roleplay it?" suggested Veronica, aka Valkyrie.

"I hate snakes, but I believe we all need to leave our pasts behind," said Megan.

"Yep, a clean slate. Now that I've been initiated, shall we have some champagne? Then I want to check out our new digs. This planet is supposed to be green and pretty, and I want a room with a big window," said Valkyrie, and left the room with the transfer chamber.

# 26. The Truth

Walter, Megan, and Sylvie followed Veronica to the kitchen. They shared some food and drank champagne. The conversation seemed light and optimistic as they made their first plans for this new colony, and even Sylvie was smiling again. While they were conversing, Walter watched them intently, and suddenly, he realized why he hadn't taken them hostage or killed them outright. It wasn't because of Megan's commitment to save him, Sylvie's nurturing care, and Veronica's intellect. No, it was because they were so darn entertaining! He raised his glass for a toast:

"To three lovely ladies who delivered an Oscar-worthy performance today. Bravo!"

Megan and Sylvie looked puzzled, but Veronica just smirked.

"Buckle up, girls. Sherlock Holmes has figured it all out," she said.

"Maybe not all, but I think I've got the gist of it. The alien program is truly amazing. I believe I could hack into the NSA, and nobody would ever know."

Sylvie still seemed confused, but Megan looked increasingly concerned.

"Veronica was mostly truthful about the other colonists. They had legal problems, were prejudiced and greedy, had addictions, anger issues, and other mental deficiencies, but that's no different from hundreds of millions of everyday people all over the world. In earthly society, their flaws had gone largely unnoticed because their neighbors, coworkers, friends, or even family members had similar or worse shortcomings. It only became a problem in the extreme setting of the colony. Without ethics, boundaries, or consequences, they were liberated from the restraints of society, which exposed and amplified their ugly yet ubiquitous characters. They didn't become savages; they always were," said Walter, and added with a smirk, "but the three of you are exceptional."

"Let's hear it, my scorpion."

"Father, mother, and daughter living in eternal youth among the stars! All that's needed are two transfer chambers, and once you grow old or sick, a 6-hour trip will fix it. I was the proof–or almost, but more about that later."

"I'm completely lost," said Sylvie, raising her eyebrows.

"Let's start with you, then. You were ill, and Ron was your boyfriend, but that's where the truth ends. You stated adamantly that you were not a slut. But you had figured out in puberty already that you wanted sex, and sex would get you everything else you needed. Simple but effective. I've counted at least a dozen different gentlemen whom you favored even before your college days. That included a couple of your high school teachers whom you seduced and then extorted for better grades. Did you know that one of them killed himself?"

Sylvie didn't respond but looked upset.

"You are an insatiable young lady, and your illness never stopped you, but Ron was left in the dark. However, when you transferred to the colony, none of your many suitors wanted to join despite your best efforts and some very explicit promises. I wonder why? So, you persuaded Ron because you didn't want to be without a man. Notwithstanding that he was secretly gay, Ron stuck with you because he truly cared for you."

"Ron was gross! He wasn't a real man."

"Perhaps, but he was one true victim, trapped by his parents and their religion and betrayed by his girlfriend. Worse yet, that swine of a doctor violated him when he was just fifteen, then threatened to tell Ron's dogmatic parents that he was gay if he didn't continue to see him. That's how Juan ended up with the colony."

Walter noticed that Veronica frowned slightly, while Megan showed no emotion, but Sylvie looked unfazed.

"But back to you, Sylvie: eventually, you found out that Ron was gay. You have kept so many secrets from him, but it pissed you off that he had kept that one secret from you. But more importantly, you had no use for him as a man anymore. That must be why you seduced me even when I was dying, and you didn't care in the slightest about dear Megan either – hmm, like mother, like daughter?"

"I didn't do that. You imagined things!" lied Sylvie, but she had missed the vital remark.

"You squealed like a stuck pig in that little restroom," interjected Veronica and laughed.

"Yes, she was quite noisy. Ron was never meant to arrive on this planet. That's why you were worried when the transfer chamber started up again after you arrived here, because you feared that your plan had gone awry. Just before you transferred, you informed Juan that Ron was going away with you, leaving him behind. That enraged Juan so much that he killed Ron. You got your revenge and no longer had to dump your boyfriend. When you witnessed his demise earlier, you put on a spectacular show of grief, strength, and resolve that would have surely fooled me if I didn't know better already."

"Oh well," mumbled Sylvie and shrugged.

"By the way, do you know that Megan isn't your aunt?"

"Megan is my mom's sister."

"So, close…," Walter began, but Megan interrupted.

"Walter, please, no!" exclaimed Megan suddenly.

"What do you mean?" wondered Sylvie.

"If the strong resemblance wasn't a clue, genetics doesn't lie. Megan is your birth mother."

"What?!" yelled Sylvie and looked at Megan.

"I was going to tell you, Sylvie. I swear it."

"Her boyfriend at the time had ditched her, and Megan didn't want to bother with a baby while her career was just taking off. She gave you up to her sister and her husband. They raised you as their own until Megan finally discovered some motherly instincts, or maybe it was just guilt, to make an appearance in your life as the caring aunt. Would you like to guess who your real daddy is?"

"Tell me!"

"The infamous Mark, of course. Unfortunately, he is currently in prison because the botched transfer messed up the timetable. I ended up with the colony instead, and the long arm of the law caught up with your daddy."

"That can't be true!" exclaimed Sylvie.

"Nadya was your name at birth, but you became Sylvie after the adoption."

"You fucking bitch! My whole life is a lie!" Sylvie screamed at Megan.

"Sylvie, I can explain..."

"Oh, shut up; you can sort that out later," said Walter and continued, "Megan and Mark never lost touch and rekindled their relationship several times, even while Megan was married to Kevin and Mark was dating Yue. But it was a rocky road because Mark didn't like to commit to anything or anyone. Kevin was a jerk and insanely jealous, but he treated Megan decently, and all her other relationships were with normal men as well. But she was obsessed with Mark, even though he treated her like crap, exploited her financially, and, at least on one occasion, sent her to the ER. Meanwhile, Megan never stopped stalking him and threatened to expose his many crooked schemes. A very toxic relationship, and I'm sure Veronica knows all the juicy details. In summary, Mark didn't want to join because he was too busy cheating his way through life. But in the end, karma was catching up with him, and he finally agreed to live among the stars with Megan and their daughter. But not with a lesbian lover, sorry little spider."

Walter looked at the redhead, but she showed no emotion.

"Ah, the lovely Veronica. You protected Megan like a mama bear and even followed her to the stars. Of course, you already suspected that Megan and Mark were a thing again. You didn't want Mark to come because he was a crook and your rival, so you manipulated Yue's thirst for vengeance. Yue messed up, and Mark wasn't killed, but the delay was enough because you knew that Mark's time was running out. With the competition behind bars, you've got a few more years with Megan."

Megan didn't speak, but Walter saw the smoldering hatred in her eyes. Meanwhile, Veronica's face still showed no expression.

"However, you learned that Megan had no intentions of bringing you along for the final leg of the journey. But you are a clever girl, and with the recording device in my prison cell, you figured out the plan. You came here to follow Megan, either to love her or to kill her, not for some carnal fun with a retiree. You toyed with a condemned man out of boredom. But your performance earlier was awe-inspiring, especially considering that you are batting for the other team."

"Guilty as charged," said Veronica and nodded.

"This finally brings us to Megan's grand plan. You had figured out the secret to immortality and eternal youth. You didn't really care about the colony because it was just a test run. That's why you didn't vet your colonists either. Ultimately, they were disposable, and you would have erased them eventually if Veronica hadn't done the work for you. After all, you only needed the chamber, not the people. It was also never a democracy because you held all the power and could have ended my captivity at any time. The alien environmental controls are quite potent - fill rooms with chlorine gas or suck out all the air, heat them up to a thousand degrees, or cool them down until the oxygen condenses out. I saw your scripts; you were well prepared for any mutiny and for the final solution."

He stopped for a moment and had a sip of champagne. The three women remained silent, but the tension in the room was palpable. Walter put the glass down and continued:

"All you really needed was the transfer chamber, and that's why you were distraught when you learned that Veronica had deconstructed the old colony. But this planet was always your final destination because it was the best one. You had found it long ago, and Mark was supposed to help you build it up. But Mark's transfer failed, and that spooked you. You didn't want to risk his life, even though he was running out of time on Earth. So, he had to go to prison, but in the long run, time didn't matter anymore since his youth could be restored. Moreover, my arrival gave you a unique research opportunity: I was old, and the radiation would make me very sick – I was the perfect lab rat."

Megan didn't show any emotions, but Sylvie still seemed furious at her mother.

"I'm still not sure why you slept with me. Was it to ensure my compliance, to piss off Kevin, or to hurt Veronica? Or were you just wet and wild and needed a good pounding since Mark hadn't made it there? Maybe all of the above?"

Megan said nothing, and Walter noticed that she didn't blush or seem uncomfortable with the sexual references. Even that had been a deception.

"Hmm, it doesn't matter. When I was near death, you sent me here. The transfer worked perfectly; I was young and healthy again, and confirmed that this planet was nice. Well, I was almost healthy, but not quite, because you didn't want me to live. You edited my DNA to include a latent flaw that would kill me within a few days, a week tops. You sent me messages every day, and when I stopped responding, you transferred here, believing that I had croaked. Your expression was priceless when you stepped over my presumably dead body, but I got up to greet you."

Megan still didn't react. Walter was impressed and simultaneously appalled by how cold-blooded that woman really was.

"With me out of the way, you and Sylvie could have the planet to yourselves until Daddy was out on parole. Sorry, Megan, I fixed that little snafu. I can live a hundred years now."

"You can't fix that!" exclaimed Megan finally.

"You cannot fix it, but I can. I knew more about the alien software in five hours than you had learned in five years. Have you ever wondered why the aliens had no medical equipment? It's because they didn't need it with the transfer chamber. If you know what you are doing, you can fix any injury or disease or even bring back the dead. Maybe I should resurrect Ron?"

"No!" shouted Sylvie impulsively, but Walter ignored her outburst and continued:

"You were right when we first met: I'm a condescending man, especially when dealing with dilettantes, but I can back it up all the way."

"I warned you, Meg. You were in way over your head with this guy," said Veronica very sweetly, but Walter sensed the venom in her words.

"Alright, ladies, here is the bottom line: get the fuck off my planet!" stated Walter and herded the three women to the transfer chamber.

"Veronica destroyed the colony. There is nowhere to go. You want to disintegrate us!" protested Megan.

"Oh, but you do have a familiar place to go, and I have already fixed it up for you. The coordinates are locked in and cannot be changed. Don't try; you will just fail again," said Walter, adding pointedly, "It was easy and took only a few hours. Competence makes all the difference, Megan."

"Walter, send them away, but you know I will do anything you like. I'll be your dirty girl again," said Sylvie, and smiled at him seductively.

"Tempting, and you are very skilled at that, but it's not up for discussion. Get moving; the transfer chamber awaits," said Walter, pointing at the alien device.

"Mr. Walter, may I talk to you in private?" asked Veronica politely.

"Mr. Walter?" he asked, but Veronica didn't answer, only smiled at him knowingly.

"You are clever. Let's step outside for a moment," replied Walter, and led her out of the room.

# 27. Exile or Safe Harbor?

He closed the door behind him and locked Megan and Sylvie in. He looked at Veronica expectantly, but the woman hesitated to speak.

"Talk!"

"Martin Walter, author of nine little-known but fascinating books. I have read one. Of course, that's just your pseudonym, and I still haven't figured out your real name. Sadly, I'm not skilled enough with the alien software to hack the copyright office."

Walter smiled a little, but didn't respond.

"I suspected that you didn't give Megan your real name, just one that was familiar to you. I knew you were educated, a scientist, and a writer. I also listened to all your conversations with Megan and Sylvie and learned that you were on the philosophical side. When I ordered all the supplies for the colony, I conducted a few searches. It took a while to narrow it down and throw out all the romance novels, religious drivel, and for-dummies books until I found you. I couldn't find any photos, addresses, biographies, or any other identifying information because you guard your privacy fiercely. So, I've read your stuff and enjoyed your warped mind, but even after just a few pages, I knew it was you. Your style betrayed you, Mr. Walter."

"I'm impressed, but that's not why you wanted to talk."

"I will be honest with you from now on. I'm lesbian and don't like men, neither their appearance nor their attitudes. I've been with Megan for over five years, but mentally, I was done with her even before you arrived. She has been a disappointment on many levels. So, I didn't mind that she slept with you and even encouraged it because you were dealt such a terrible hand. We were never rivals."

Veronica paused for a moment before she continued:

"I was also aware of how she felt about Mark and suspected that Sylvie was their daughter. I was willing to share her with Mark, even sleep with that scumbag if that was required, but Megan used and discarded me, and I'm too fucking proud to let that slide. Please let me stay with you."

"Veronica, with you around, I would have to watch my back every second of every day. You are too smart and too dangerous."

"Imprison me. Beat me. Rape me whenever you want. I will always comply, but please let me stay!" begged the redhead.

"You know I wouldn't abuse you," said Walter, and added with a frown, "but I never imagined you would be so submissive. It doesn't suit you."

"What's my choice? If I go with Megan, she, Mark, or Sylvie will kill me if the humiliation doesn't kill me first. I'd rather die here with you."

Veronica dropped to her knees and bowed her head. Walter looked at her for a moment. He bent down and extended his hand. She looked at him with tears in her eyes and took it.

"Fine. We can share this planet. Maybe we can become friends someday."

"No, I don't want to be friends," said Veronica, and shook her head.

"Well, roommates or neighbors then."

"You misunderstood. I want to be with you, always. I don't care that you are a man. You are still my needle, and I'm yours. That was always true, Mr. Walter."

"The name is Tiberius, Valkyrie."

"Tiberius. Roman Empire?"

"Yes, my father was a historian."

"I like it, and thank you for calling me Valkyrie again."

"Sure, we should probably discuss some rules now."

"Yes, Tiberius, but can we have sex first?"

"Seriously? That again?" he asked with apparent disdain in his voice.

"I'm serious and not flirting with you," said Valkyrie, and added, "We need this, and you know that."

Tiberius was silent for a while. Valkyrie's ridiculous request had caught him off guard. She was a lesbian and had deceived and manipulated him. Why would he sleep with this woman?

"Explain."

"You cared for Megan. You hide it, but you are as hurt as I am. We have to kill that pain to move on."

"I wasn't hurt by Megan."

"Yes, you were. You made it a point to humiliate Megan where it stings the most: her intellect," said Valkyrie, and added, "I approved wholeheartedly."

Tiberius knew that Valkyrie was right. He was hurt by Megan's deceit, and that's why he had lashed out. Still, it would be a costly mistake to be intimate with Veronica because she was gorgeous and, even more importantly to him, brilliant. If he slept with her, it would likely create some kind of bond. Not for her, of course, but probably for him, and she could and would exploit that. But against his better judgment, Tiberius knew that he would give in to her advances sooner or later.

"If I sleep with you, do me one favor: don't pretend that you like it so much that you've changed your sexual orientation. I would never believe it, and it would make me avoid you for the next hundred years or for however long we will live."

Valkyrie has heard the 'you are only a lesbian because you haven't been with me' bullshit a hundred times in her life, but Tiberius was the exact opposite: he desired her but knew that it would always be a one-way street. Valkyrie was fascinated and silently vowed to enjoy this new game.

"What if I really like it? Do I have to lie?"

"That's nonsense, but don't lie. I would hate that even more."

"You were right; all my flirting was just a façade. I toyed with you and enjoyed it, but didn't do it to torment a dying man. You were a prisoner in that room, but my prison was only slightly bigger. I was depressed and needed the banter. I appreciate that you played along because it made it a little easier for me, and I hoped that it made the bad situation a tiny bit better for you, too."

"It did," admitted Tiberius and nodded slightly.

"I have been with men, but sexually, they do nothing for me. However, I like you as a person. That wasn't a lie, Tiberius. But for whatever reason, your description of the fight between the spider and the scorpion turned me on. Ever since, I have wondered what it would be like to be with you. That's the truth, and I swear it."

"Hmm, we'll find out soon, little spider," replied Tiberius, chuckled, and shook his head.

"Thank you," said Valkyrie softly.

Tiberius left Valkyrie and entered the transfer room again. Sylvie had departed already, but Megan was still there, sitting next to the console. She looked defiantly at him.

"You are keeping that psycho who killed a bunch of people, but you are sending me away?" asked Megan, and added forcefully, "I was nice to you, Walter!"

"That's a strange definition of nice," replied Tiberius and added sternly, "Leave or perish."

"You talk tough, but you don't have it in you. All those principles and ethics made you weak," said Megan, and continued, "You sneered at us because we wanted to look beautiful, but you should have taken my offer to make your cock bigger. Mark is ten times the man you are!"

Tiberius laughed out loud at the juvenile insult, but he was internally repulsed by both her and himself. How could he have missed that Megan was such a deplorable person?

"In ten minutes, the transfer chamber will be absorbed by the structure. Then the room will fill with water all the way to the ceiling, and I won't drain it again until tomorrow," said Tiberius and asked rhetorically, "Perhaps you wouldn't be in this situation if you had improved your brain instead of your tits?"

He pointed once more at the alien device, then left the room and locked the door. He thought about Valkyrie again and second-guessed his decision to let her stay. If he woke up with a knife in his back tomorrow, he had nobody else to blame. She had an unknown agenda, and Tiberius had no illusions: if Valkyrie stayed here, he would die at her hands eventually. He needed to prepare a failsafe urgently. But a part of him still liked the tall redhead, even if that turned out to be a fatal mistake.

Tiberius returned to the kitchen. Valkyrie was having another glass of champagne. She put the glass on the counter and gently wrapped her arms around his neck. For a moment, she just looked into his eyes and smiled. Then she kissed him softly on the lips, and her hand went to his groin. He lifted her up by her waist and set her down on the counter. She opened her legs for him, then closed them behind his back. They made love like that for quite a while. Tiberius enjoyed it a lot, and Valkyrie was engaged, but he sensed that she didn't share his enthusiasm.

Tiberius felt much better after sex and silently admitted that she had been right: he was hurt and needed to get that out of his system. Sweet and caring Sylvie knew Ron for half of her life, but had been merciless to her gay boyfriend. But Valkyrie, the cold and calculating lesbian, was so empathetic to a straight man she barely knew. Tiberius wasn't entirely sure of her motives and might still be dead wrong, but he resolved that Valkyrie deserved some credit.

"What would your perfect woman look like?" asked Tiberius after they had finished.

"Young, but not too young, tall like me with long legs, blue eyes, long wavy black hair, soft facial features, a shapely figure, perfect teeth, and lush lips," replied Valkyrie immediately.

Tiberius presumed that she had accurately described her ideal lover. He made a mental note of that, then poured her another glass of champagne and quipped:

"Lush lips? Which ones?"

"All of them, naughty boy," replied Valkyrie, laughing, and asked, "What's your ideal woman?"

"You are exquisite and exceed all my physical criteria. Your green eyes are stunning, but what truly arouses me is what's behind them."

"You judge more by the inside than the outside. That's healthy, but uncommon."

"To really enjoy it, I have to find the woman intellectually attractive too."

"You fucked my mind, not my body?" she asked bluntly with a broad grin.

"Both, and thank you for playing along. It probably wasn't easy for you."

"It was not hard at all, and we needed to get this out of the way," was her business-like reply.

"Of course."

"That came out wrong. I will sleep with you again, Tibs."

"I'll keep that in mind," he said, kissed her on the cheek, and added, "Let me show you your room. It has a window, but it's pretty small. The aliens didn't have windows, and I had to improvise."

"Wait, you didn't know I was coming here, and then you were going to send me away. Why did you make a room for me?"

"I knew that you would follow Megan. I was always going to exile Megan and Sylvie, but there was a small chance that you might stay. I prepared a room, just in case. You'll find some reading material there. You had included one of my books in your deliveries, and I hope you'll enjoy it."

"You are full of surprises," said Valkyrie, shaking her head before she added, "Alright, show me my prison."

"Oh, you are free to go anywhere you like. I won't keep you locked up, Val."

"Val?" she repeated with a sly smile.

"If you call me Tibs, I'll call you Val."

"You still like me," she said, beaming a warm smile at him.

"I probably won't like you by tomorrow morning when my skull is cracked open."

"I prefer to kill in more hands-off ways. Blood and gore aren't my style."

"Good to know," he said with a smirk and added, "Now get some rest. Tomorrow, we'll discuss the house rules."

"I don't deserve leniency, but I appreciate it more than you will ever know. I will never hurt you. Goodnight, Tibs," said Valkyrie and kissed his cheek.

"One more thing: if you change your mind, just tell me. I will send you to where Megan is going or give you your own planet if you prefer that," said Tiberius, and added with a thin smile, "Goodnight, Val."

He left Val's room and checked the logs on the laptop. Megan had finally transferred, but he wouldn't have cared if she hadn't. Tiberius reprogrammed the environmental controls and drained the water from that room.

# 28. Good Company

Valkyrie did not change her mind, and the next couple of months were surprisingly harmonious. Valkyrie and Tiberius synergized on almost every level. They discussed very personal things and learned about each other's histories. For Tiberius, it was a novel experience: when he spoke to Valkyrie, she didn't respond with a blank stare. He didn't have to repeat himself or dumb down the language. She understood him, and the few times when she didn't, she asked good questions and raptly listened to his answers. He did the same when she spoke. Perhaps for the first time in his life, Tiberius could converse like an adult, and he appreciated that more than anything else.

Valkyrie and Tiberius worked together, had their meals together, and laughed together. Tiberius never thought of the redheaded woman as a homemaker, but she turned the barren, alien complex into a cozy retreat. Not a day passed that she didn't zap some packages from Earth to make it a little better. Meanwhile, Tiberius was the handyman, fixing whatever broke, needed improvement, or required assembly. The window in Valkyrie's room was huge now, and she had a stunning view of a lively brook, a field of colorful flowers, and the tall mountains in the distance.

They still had no clothes but didn't mind being naked around each other. Eventually, they acquired a couple of overalls for the outside, one suit for Tiberius, and a beautiful cocktail dress for Valkyrie, along with matching shoes. They never wore formal clothes until they had some music and converted one of the many empty rooms into a dancefloor. Val was a good dancer, but Tiberius hadn't done it in 40 years, so he was pretty rusty. He must have stepped on her toes a million times and probably moved around like Sasquatch, but they had so much fun that it became a weekly activity. On other days, they played board or card games, or simply sat outside at night and watched the stars in silence. When the weather was sunny and calm, they would play badminton on a makeshift court in front of the complex. They had individual hobbies, too: Tiberius was busy writing a new book, and Valkyrie was painting for many hours at a time.

But almost every day, they chose a topic or a book for discussion. Often, their talks were quite contentious and passionate. They challenged each other fiercely, but neither took any offense, and the debates ended harmoniously. Tiberius had never met anyone like Val, and she seemed to love his company just as much. He admitted that Valkyrie was the one sharp needle in the monumental haystack of ignorance, so it was no surprise that Tiberius quickly grew very fond of her, and the feeling seemed mutual. Life was good for them, and to any observer, they would have looked like the perfect couple. But they did not sleep together.

Tiberius enjoyed these days but was also wary. He had watched Val closely but couldn't detect any deceit. But she was extraordinary and had already proven to be a gifted actress, so he decided to confront her directly.

"Val, we need to have a serious talk."

"I know what's coming. Go ahead, Tibs."

"It made sense that you didn't want to join Megan because your life would be in danger. Cutting your losses and staying here was the rational choice. But even though I enjoy your company, I wonder what your endgame is since you cannot return to Earth or the old colony?"

"I expected that question. What do you believe it is?"

"I don't know, that's why I'm asking."

"Is it not conceivable that I just want to be here with you?"

"It is conceivable but improbable."

"Why is it improbable?" asked Valkyrie and raised her eyebrows.

"There are good reasons, and you know that," said Tiberius.

"Name them."

"Struggle for intellectual supremacy, sexual orientation, difference in true age, and socialization or lack thereof are the main ones," said Tiberius and asked, "Val, just be honest with me, and we will try to find an acceptable solution together."

"If I say I don't care about our differences, would you accept that?"

"I would have no choice but to believe you since I cannot disprove it. You are a master manipulator, and that's not criticism because I respect your skill. But as I said before, that makes you very dangerous."

"You have trust issues, Tibs."

"Trust is an irrational concept. I can choose whom to betray, but I have no control over others who do it to me. Instead of trusting, I prefer to estimate the odds of betrayal. They are never 100%, but can also never be zero. Furthermore, under the right circumstances and with the proper incentives, everyone is capable of betrayal or worse," said Tibs and added, "We are a product of our experiences, and perhaps mine haven't been that great, but I'm not an idiot to repeat the same mistakes over and over again, hoping for different results."

"What are the odds that I will betray you?"

"I don't have a precise number, but they are high."

"You believe that I'm patiently waiting for the perfect moment to kill you?"

"Yes, but I'm trying to avoid that scenario because I wouldn't want to kill you."

"Why not?"

"If I kill you, our game ends. A few moments of horror, and then it's all over, and you haven't even learned a lesson."

"But you would have the satisfaction of winning!" she exclaimed, and Tiberius noticed that it excited her.

"I'm not that interested in winning because it's actually boring to me."

"Boring? Because you always win?"

"Because I'll be disappointed when the game ends."

"Disappointed that your opponent was too weak?"

"I usually give my opponent some credit unless they have insulted my intelligence with their schemes."

"Like Megan?"

"Yes, like Megan. I gave her credit for the deception, but her plan could have been drawn up by a preschooler."

"I understood why you spared Sylvie. She was ruthless and a slave to her urges, but she was nice to you. But Megan? Why didn't you kill her?"

"Too many people are woefully ignorant. They are incapable of accepting responsibility for their actions and instead will double down on cheap excuses, lies, denial, or blaming others. Those could be killed because they will never learn a goddam thing. But Megan is smart. Not smart enough to be a threat, but enough to realize her mistakes. Her life depends on my mercy, where she is now. I could kill her in a million different ways – tomorrow, next month, or ten years from now – she knows that, but cannot do anything about it. Naturally, she hates me, but perhaps she can learn a lesson in time?"

"A fitting punishment, but I would have just killed her. That was my plan when I came here," said Val, and returned to the previous topic, "the only answer I have for you is this: if you don't trust me, send me away, imprison or kill me."

"Hmm."

"You claim that you enjoy my company, yet you are pushing me away," said Valkyrie, and frowned.

"For both of our sakes," said Tiberius, and concluded the conversation, "Thanks for the talk, Val."

Tiberius didn't expect this exchange to yield anything actionable, but it confirmed something concerning: Val might enjoy his company, but she was still playing to win, whatever that meant to her.

# 29. Tensions

Today, just like every morning for the last three months, Tiberius made breakfast for both of them. Valkyrie greeted him with a kiss on the cheek after she woke up and came to the kitchen. He served her a plate with toasted waffles and a cup of freshly brewed coffee, the real thing from Earth, not the stuff from the alien food processor.

"I expected to be imprisoned, maybe beaten and occasionally raped, not treated like a queen," said Val with a broad smile when she took the steaming mug from his hands.

"If you prefer, we could still arrange for that?" quipped Tiberius.

"I'm the only woman on the planet, and I told you that I would comply. Why aren't you raping me?" asked Val provocatively.

"I'm not sure if you are serious or just pushing my buttons," said Tiberius, and continued, "Intimacy isn't about me; it's about her. Maybe that's not how most men think, but I wouldn't and couldn't rape you. Frankly, I'm a little offended that you even ask that."

"I'm sorry, Tibs. It was in bad taste," she said, and asked, "What would you do if I were not here?"

"Oh, maybe I would go hiking and explore this new world, or study the aliens and their technology more thoroughly, and find out who they were and why they are gone."

"Be honest, do you regret letting me stay here?"

"No, since you haven't killed me yet," said Tiberius and grinned at her.

"Oh yeah, I forgot again. I'll put a reminder on the fridge," replied Val and nodded.

She got up from the table and walked to the fridge. They had a to-do list posted there, and she added 'Kill Tibs' but dotted the i's with little hearts. Tiberius was laughing and shook his head.

"We get along so well, and I love your dark humor. I have no regrets at all, Val."

"We are a great match because we are the same kind of crazy," said Val with a smile, and added, "Sad to think that we would have never met on Earth. I didn't frequent the establishments of geriatric geniuses, and you wouldn't be hanging out with the dykes at the club."

"As you said, we are needles in a haystack. But I'm insane, so maybe I would have been your patient?"

"Pfft, you would be the last person to show up for therapy," joked Val and changed the topic, "If I weren't here, would you get yourself a pretty girl from Earth?"

"No."

"Why not?"

"I don't kidnap people and hold them prisoner."

"But she might like it here, and she might like you," said Val, and added, "You are everything a straight woman would want in a man."

"I would be no better than a rapist," said Tiberius, and asked, "Val, why do you think so poorly of me today? Have I offended you?"

"I've never once thought poorly of you, Tibs. You are what every human should be like," said Val and smiled at him fondly before she added very bluntly, "but you have needs and can't go down to the local bar to pick up some drunk chick or pay a few bucks for a blowjob in the backseat of your car. You don't even have a goat here."

Tiberius had to laugh out loud. Valkyrie wasn't vulgar, but she used vulgarity to make a point, and he had to admit that it had the desired effect. She was crude, but that made her unambiguous.

"May I remind you that you are in the same boat as me?" noted Tiberius rhetorically and asked sarcastically, "Would you like me to abduct a pretty girl for you?"

"You would do that for me?" she replied with feigned excitement.

"I wouldn't abduct anyone, but if you have a lady friend who wants to come here, we can arrange for that," said Tiberius.

"But you wouldn't do that for yourself?"

"I've burned all my bridges a long time ago. Nobody would come."

"Yeah, I've burned mine too," she said and shrugged her shoulders before asking, "So, you would spend the rest of your life alone?"

"If that's the hand I was dealt, I would do that," said Tiberius and nodded.

"Hmm, I guess you really would. I'm not sure if I could do that."

"But for better or worse, I still have you. Misery loves company, Val," he said with a thin smile.

But Valkyrie didn't seem to appreciate the playful comment. Something was off with her today, and Tiberius wondered what it might be.

"You pride yourself on being rational and logical even under the direst circumstances."

"I wouldn't say that I'm proud of it, but I try to be rational."

"You are as irrational as the rest of us, and I can prove it," said Val sharply.

"I'm listening."

"You are healthy, virile, and in your prime. You believe you have your urges under control, but in a few months, sex is all you can think of because you are marooned on this alien planet with no reprieve. Yet you kicked out the two women you've slept with, and who would have been eager to do the mother-daughter fantasy for you, in favor of a lesbian psycho who possibly kills you someday. Does that sound rational to you?"

"That hurts, Val."

But Tiberius knew that Val was right. He let her stay because he liked her, and sent Megan and Sylvie away because he didn't like them. Those were emotional decisions, and when he made them, he didn't think of any consequences. Val had hit a nerve, but Tibs wasn't upset with her. No, quite the contrary - he admired her sharp mind!

"We are the only two people on this planet. I've been here for nearly three months, but you never asked me to sleep with you. Will you ever ask?" she asked, and he noticed the edge in her voice.

"No, I won't ask you, Val."

"Why not?" she pressed on.

"Do you really want an answer to that question?"

"Yes, really! Spit it out!" she demanded loudly.

Tiberius never had an argument with Valkyrie before and didn't fully understand what was happening there. He must have offended her somehow and considered just walking away to let her cool down, but she had hit a sore spot, and it annoyed him.

"Val, you are not bisexual; you are a lesbian and don't like men. I still don't understand why you had sex with me after I let you stay!" stated Tiberius pointedly.

"On Earth, you would have been on your own, but this is not Earth!" she replied angrily.

"Was it gratitude, fear, or pity?" he asked with a frown.

"Fuck you, Tibs! I was grateful and still am. But I did it because you were hurt and needed it. I don't care about men, but I care about you, now and always!" shouted Val and glared at him with her piercing green eyes.

The talk had escalated so quickly, and he could tell that she was furious now. Val's strong reaction took him by surprise, but he was sorry for his comment. Because of her nonchalant, cerebral attitude and all the morbid humor, it was hard to think of Val as empathic. But she was empathic, possibly more than most people. However, she showed it in the most unusual ways.

"I appreciate that and apologize," said Tiberius sincerely.

"I know you are frustrated, and I'm sorry too," said Val, and asked, "You don't regret letting me stay, but would you prefer if I were not here?"

"You know how much I enjoy your company, but it also makes it harder for me at times."

"A naked man is at a disadvantage. I can tell when you get aroused," said Val bluntly and added with a smirk, "and then you quickly disappear into the bathroom."

"Damn, I knew we should have had a dress code," replied Tiberius humorously, but embarrassed that she had noticed.

"You want to sleep with me, but you think that sex is about the woman, not you. You won't ask because you know that I don't enjoy it much."

"That, and because I respect you. I don't want to use you like a whore. Unfortunately, there is no solution to this problem," said Tiberius, but Valkyrie did not reply and remained silent for several minutes.

"You said you could give me my own planet?" she finally asked.

Tiberius was saddened by that question, but he understood the sentiment behind it. This whole conversation made a lot more sense now. Valkyrie has become uncomfortable with him. He would miss her greatly, but wouldn't stop her from leaving. It was so nice while it lasted, but perhaps it was time to go their separate ways?

"I can do that, but the selection is minimal. I've found only two decent candidates, three if you want to go back to the original colony."

"How quickly could you build a complex?"

"I could duplicate this one with a few minor modifications, and it will take only a few hours," said Tiberius, and asked, "If I start now, you can transfer there after dinner. Do you want that?"

"Hmm," was all she said, and Tiberius realized that life would be harsh for her on a new world.

"The new complex would be barren. It's better if I transfer instead."

"And just like that, everything we have would be lost after the last supper?" asked Valkyrie, raising her eyebrows.

"Val, you were right earlier. Every time I look at you, I think about sex. I know that's disrespectful, and I sincerely apologize. If I were still an old man, it would be much easier to ignore those damn desires. I forgot how powerful that was when I was young. It made me do stupid things back then, and it's doing it again now. You are unhappy because I creep you out. Additionally, you must contend with your own unfulfilled needs. I wish I could fix that, but I'm unable to do so. Hence, I will do whatever alleviates the situation and start working on the new complex right away."

"No, I just wanted to see if you would do it," she replied and smiled fondly at him.

"You tested me? Of course, I would do that for you!" he stated firmly.

"Tibs, you are not leaving, and I'm not leaving unless you kick me out."

"If you leave, you leave of your own accord. I will never kick you out."

For a while, they didn't say anything. Tiberius was cleaning the kitchen counter, and Val was finishing her coffee. She put the cup down and refilled it, then spoke again:

"We are too smart, too proud, and too stubborn to fit in with humanity. That's why we are stuck on this planet together. A dyke and an old-school gentleman in the strangest marriage of all time. It's a good marriage, but something has to change."

"What do you propose?"

"If you don't ask me for sex, I will ask you."

"That's sweet but also ridiculous."

"It's not ridiculous, and don't say that. We have a relationship, even if it's a weird one, and in a relationship, you give and take," said Val, and added forcefully, "I know you would give me everything, even my own planet, so let me do something for you!"

Valkyrie stood up from the table and walked behind the counter where he was standing. Tiberius remained silent but considered her words carefully. He hadn't thought of them as a couple, but Valkyrie had a point: they had a relationship, and he would do whatever he could to make her happy.

"You are not wrong, Val," he conceded with a sigh and rinsed out his coffee mug.

"But?"

Valkyrie was everything Tiberius ever wanted in a woman, physically and intellectually. But if he slept with her, the dynamics would become lopsided because of his desires. Val would hold the power in their relationship, and equality would be lost. Of course, she knew that too, and perhaps that's why she was so adamant about intimacy. It was a lose-lose situation for Tiberius, but he was impressed by how skillfully she had navigated the circumstances to get to this point.

"One moment," said Tibs, then walked to the fridge and scribbled 'Rape Val' with a smiley face on the to-do list.

Val read it and laughed out loud, but then pointed at the list and said in the voice of an irate wife:

"Get to it, honey!"

# 30. The Garden

Tiberius studied the aliens almost every day. And nearly every day, he discovered something new and fascinating. He learned how the large balls of Play-Doh ended up on the planets: they were not dropped there or built on the surface; they were seeded. The relay sent a tiny sample to the surface, and then it grew inside the soil, much like a mushroom, utilizing the planet's natural resources to expand. It even created a power source inside its underground stem, and as the last step, all the alien machinery, including the transfer chamber. The aliens used a different time scale, but he estimated that the process was surprisingly fast. The big ball was created in a matter of only a few months.

The aliens had standardized the procedure so that each ball had the correct dimensions for their dens. However, Tiberius discovered that these parameters could be changed. The seed could grow to an immense size, comparable to a skyscraper or even an entire city, as long as the planet provided enough raw materials. But it could also remain as small as a tool shed, with most of its structure deep underground. If he had to return to Earth someday, this might be the way to do it relatively inconspicuously.

The other significant discovery was that the transfer chamber could alter the appearance to a much greater extent than just skin-deep beauty, but there were a few limitations. Tiberius could transmute into a dog, a cat, a raven, or possibly even a gorilla, but not an elephant, because the pod was not large enough to accommodate such a size. He could even become a mythical figure like an elf, a dwarf, or an orc.

He also discovered that the chamber could act as both a sender and a receiver simultaneously. He could enter the contraption and, six hours later, exit it as the tooth fairy, provided that he created a proper genetic profile for that. Lastly, Tiberius discovered that the aliens actually used the device to duplicate themselves. He thought it would be unsettling to have another Tiberius around, but apparently, the aliens had no ethical or practical concerns, as their hivemind mentality valued the whole, not the individual.

Tiberius and Valkyrie had turned a patch of land in front of the complex into a vegetable garden, complete with irrigation and a fence to keep the native wildlife out. The creatures on this planet were docile and didn't bother them, but they liked the earthly flora. The bounty from the garden was much tastier than anything that the alien food processor could make. Today, they were harvesting tomatoes for the first time. Val was humming a tune while she checked if the fruits were ripe. Tibs followed her with a big basket to collect whatever she selected.

"Val, could you love Megan again?" he asked.

"No! Don't send me there!" exclaimed Val suddenly, dropped a tomato, and looked at him, concerned.

"Oh, I would never do that, and that's not why I'm asking," replied Tibs reassuringly.

Val picked up the dropped tomato and put it in his basket. She looked at him again and smiled slyly.

"Let me guess, you think a bisexual woman could solve our problems?"

"Well, perhaps."

"I know you so well," teased Val, but then added more seriously, "When Megan wanted sex, she didn't care who or what got her off. I think she would have banged her Labrador when she got into the mood. Don't get me wrong: the sex was great, and probably for you too, but I wouldn't call Megan bisexual. She was just a selfish bitch when she got horny."

Tiberius remembered that it felt like rape when Megan slept with him for the second time. Val was probably right about Megan, but he could also tell that she still harbored unresolved anger. She had taken his pain away, but he couldn't do the same for her, and it saddened him.

"How did you hook up with her?"

"Right after Kevin had left her, she became my patient. We talked; she looked fine, and I liked her because she was astute. I just got dumped by my girlfriend a few weeks earlier, so Megan and I went out to drown our sorrows and ended up in bed. I thought that was it, but Megan wanted more. Even back then, I feared that she couldn't be trusted. But unlike you, I don't have a selection of 4 billion women, so I took what I could get. We continued dating, and she spent a lot of time at my house. We even went on vacations together. Call me an idiot, but I fell in love with her despite the red flags."

"I understand, and thanks for telling me."

"But back to your idea: we find a bisexual chick and take turns or have a threesome. We fuck the hell out of her and go on with our lives. It's a fun idea, and I'm all for it if this were Earth. But this isn't Earth, and you are not thinking long-term again. Here, a bisexual woman will inevitably align herself with you or with me. She might even exploit that if she's devious. We could become rivals, and everything we have goes down the drain over some pussy. I don't want that."

"A good point, and I don't want that either," conceded Tiberius and asked, "Val, would you like to return to Earth?"

"Could you do that?"

"It won't be fast or easy because I would have to build a new transfer chamber in a decent place, and there is no guarantee that it will work. Would you like me to try that?" Tiberius asked, but Valkyrie didn't reply for some time.

"If you come with me, I'll go. But you won't go, right?"

"No, I wouldn't," said Tiberius and added, "There is no place for me on Earth anymore, but you could live a full life there."

"I know what you are trying to do and appreciate that, but it infuriates me. You would sacrifice everything for me. It's too much, don't do that," said Val, and added, "If you go to Earth, I'll come with you. If you stay here, I'll stay here too. We are a package deal - is that so hard to understand?"

"OK, I'll try to get both of us to Earth."

"Imagine what we could do with the alien tech on Earth together! We could be billionaires, you could be president, and I'll be your trophy wife. We'll live like royalty, perhaps like gods, adored and worshipped by a horde of blithering fools if we just appeal to their most savage instincts. And if we screw them, they'll just love us even more because they are too stupid to know better. We could mess with the whole world and shape it to our liking or destroy it for fun."

"That's the narcissist in you speaking, Val. I'm not like you in that regard."

"You wouldn't enjoy toying with them?"

"I went through three phases in my life once I discovered how different I was. When I was a teenager, I used my gifts to manipulate others, and I found it amusing. But I got bored because it was too easy. During the next phase, I thought I could teach others to be better, but it frustrated me to no end because most cannot be better and don't even want to try."

"And the last phase?"

"That's me now. I have no desire to interact with the blithering fools because they disgust me to the point that I lose my appetite," said Tiberius, but conceded with a sigh, "However, we can go to Earth together and mess with it if that makes you happy. Who knows, maybe I will develop a taste for power again?"

Valkyrie thought about this for a while, and Tiberius could tell that she was intrigued by that idea. But eventually, she looked at him and shook her head.

"No, you love to be here on this planet with me. This is our home. Earth sucks, and we will not go back there. That's final!" said Valkyrie resolutely.

"Yes, Ma'am!" replied Tiberius humorously and changed the topic, "The aliens used the transfer chamber very differently: they duplicated themselves."

"They made clones?" wondered Val and rechecked the vines.

"No, not clones, but duplicates: identical in body and mind. It might be unethical by human standards, but I could duplicate Megan for you."

"Stop it, I don't want Megan!" stated Val with a frown and asked snidely, "Why don't you duplicate your dirty girl?"

Tibs didn't reply, but her comment annoyed him. He would rather be celibate than create another Sylvie. Val noticed his reaction and shook her head.

"That was mean," she said and then asked curiously, "Could you make any other woman?"

"The machine can only create what's stored in its memory. As you said, I could duplicate Sylvie. I could make a female body with a blank brain like a fully grown baby, or…"

"Or what?"

"I could duplicate you."

"What?" asked Val, and stopped harvesting.

"The chamber could make another Valkyrie or even a dozen of you."

"That's a whole new dimension of narcissism," she said, but he noticed that she was amused by the concept.

"You are smart, fun, and very helpful around the complex. I wouldn't mind another one of you," quipped Tiberius, but Valkyrie didn't think it was funny.

"But I would mind!" stated Val sternly and asked, "Why are you turning the tables on me?"

"Because I know you are sexually frustrated, and unlike me, you have no outlet," said Tiberius, and added quietly, "It's unfair and breaks my heart, Val."

"Do you remember when I suggested that you should rape me or kidnap some cute chick from Earth? How did that make you feel?"

"I was offended."

"I said that because I wanted you to be happy, but then realized that my depraved suggestions hurt more than they helped," said Val, and added forcefully, "You are doing the same thing now!"

"You are right, and I'm very sorry," he apologized, adding, "You are stronger than I am."

"Bullshit. You could live the rest of your life without anybody. You don't need me, I need you."

"No, I don't think I could do that anymore," he said softly.

"Oh? Not five minutes ago, you wanted to ship me off to Earth."

"I know and would have done it. But I'm glad that you rejected that idea. I would be miserable without you," said Tiberius, and added quietly, "Please don't pretend that you wouldn't do the same for me."

Val stopped picking tomatoes. She looked so sad now, and Tibs noticed immediately. He put his arm around her shoulders and kissed her head.

"This planet is serene and beautiful. We are Adam and Eve in the Garden of Eden."

"That's a fitting analogy."

"Except Eve has a problem," she said and sighed.

"Val, no! You were born this way, and you are perfect. Don't ever question that," said Tiberius, and added strongly, "If I had the choice between the most amazing straight woman and you, I would choose you every single time!"

"We are not just finishing each other's sentences; we think each other's thoughts and feel each other's emotions. We would kill and die for each other. I never thought it was possible to be so close to another person," said Val, and added with tears in her eyes, "You are everything to me, but I can't be everything to you."

"You are everything to me, too. Promise me that you won't give up."

"I will never give up on you," said Val and quipped, "Perhaps in 10 years or so, I'll be a normal chick and pop out your babies?"

"You are so funny, and I wouldn't want you any other way," said Tiberius with a big grin, but Val was still very serious.

"I considered that," she said quietly.

"Considered what?"

"Getting pregnant. Maybe it helps?"

"I never had kids, but I would want your child. However, I doubt that it would fix our little problem and fear that it might make it worse."

Valkyrie didn't respond. She wiped her tears away and looked at him fondly, then shook her head and started to pluck tomatoes again.

# 31. Happy Birthday

They had lived on the new planet for nine months now, and Tiberius loved it. The isolation and serenity might not work for most people, but for him, it was so much better than Earth. He got up early in the mornings, tackled a bunch of tasks, had regular meals, and spent a lot of time with Valkyrie in the evenings. Life was simple, but it had a purpose. But today, he got up much earlier because it was Valkyrie's birthday. He silently went to the kitchen, decorated it a little, and left a card for her on the counter.

When Valkyrie woke up and went for breakfast, she smiled. The coffee was ready, there was a cake with some candles on the dining table, and a few balloons by the chair where she usually sat. She also found a bottle of champagne in the fridge. Then she saw the card on the counter, opened it, and read it.

*Happy Birthday, Val!*

*You are the best thing that has ever happened to me. I'm so glad you stayed here. Enjoy the cake. I will be back soon with your gift.*

*Tibs*

Valkyrie had some cake with a cup of coffee. She was reading the news on Earth, but it was crappy as usual, and she put the tablet down. Valkyrie wasn't big on celebrating her birthdays, but she wondered where Tibs had gone today and what kind of surprise he would bring back for her. While enjoying the coffee, Val reflected on her life. Tiberius was gentle, honest, and stimulated her intellect in ways that nobody had ever done before. They laughed a lot, had deep conversations, played the most delightful mind games, and she knew that he loved her even though he had never told her that. They were intimate quite often because Tibs needed that. However, although he tried his very best, he was a man, and it was never gratifying for her, which made him feel guilty.

Suddenly, her tablet pinged. She checked and was immediately alarmed. The alien program announced that a transfer was complete, and the person was about to wake up. That was disturbing because it shouldn't be happening. The only people who could transfer here were Megan and Sylvie, and if they did, that was bad news. Valkyrie stood up, grabbed the longest, sharpest kitchen knife, and ran to the transfer room.

When she got there, the lid of the chamber was just opening. A naked woman climbed out and smiled at her. Valkyrie feared that it would be Megan, but the woman looked different and very beautiful. No, not just lovely - she was perfect: about 25 years old, tall with long legs, blue eyes, long wavy black hair, soft facial features, a shapely figure, perfect teeth, and lush lips. Valkyrie stared at her for almost a minute before she recognized the resemblance.

"Tibs?" she stammered.

"Happy Birthday, Val," he replied fondly, surprised by the melodious, feminine sound of his voice.

"Oh, my goodness!" was all she could say before she dropped the knife and rushed to hug him fiercely.

"Do you like your gift?"

"I love it, but why?"

"You endured my affections for months and more often than you should have. I wanted to give something back to you."

Tiberius was a straight male with a strong personality. There was nothing queer about him, and he wasn't confused about his sexuality or gender. He became a woman solely for her benefit, and that was almost too much of a gift to accept.

"That's a huge sacrifice, and I didn't endure anything," she said and kissed him - or her - deeply.

"I can change back and might do that someday, but now it's your turn to get what you want," said Tibs.

Val didn't respond for a while. She seemed overwhelmed by her emotions, and Tiberius gave her some time to recover.

"It doesn't matter if you are a man, a woman, or a damn octopus. I still want to fuck you because of who you are," she whispered in his ear.

"Tentacle sex? That's kinky. Maybe we can try that someday?" he quipped, and she giggled a little.

"You are just the most amazing person," Val said, wiping away some tears.

"You are amazing, too, my little spider. Shall we have some champagne?"

"Yes, let's get drunk and freaky!" she exclaimed, laughing out loud.

"But you have to show me how to be a woman. I'm a newbie at that."

"Oh, I'll show you, alright!" said Valkyrie and winked at Tibs.

Lovemaking was exhilarating and lasted for a couple of hours. Tiberius had a lot to learn, but Val was a patient teacher. He loved how excited and aroused she was. He had never seen her so happy, and it made everything worthwhile. After they had finished, they continued to lie in each other's arms. Tiberius thought that the experience had been new and pleasurable, but somewhat different for a woman than it had been for a man. He still preferred to be a man, perhaps just because it was more familiar, but he was enjoying this change and would remain a woman for as long as Val needed that. Valkyrie seemed deeply satisfied and snuggled closer to him.

"I've never asked you before: where did you send Megan and Sylvie?"

"Earth, of course."

"I thought that wasn't possible?"

"Earth had a big ball of Play-Doh, too, but it was hidden under the ice. Megan was aware of it, but couldn't figure out how to make it work under those conditions. I created a complex inside the ice sheet, but it has an exit to go outside if they know how to shovel snow. The weather is a bit rough in Antarctica, but the penguins can keep them company until someone finds them someday."

"When I got the message that a transfer was in progress, I feared that they were coming back."

"They cannot. Their transfer chamber can only receive people but not send them out again. Mark could join them when he's out of prison, but it's a permanent one-way street."

"Are they enhanced?"

"No, they are the way they were on Earth, but young, and Sylvie isn't ill anymore."

"That's merciful," said Val and asked, "How did you master the software so quickly when everyone else was struggling with it for years?"

"Megan's approach was very scientific but incredibly slow and cumbersome. I could have gone the same route, but I'm too lazy for that. So, I tried to think like the aliens, and fortunately, that worked."

"You are not lazy."

"I'm a sloth. Rather than working hard, I prefer to work smart and then take a little nap."

"I guess that works when you are a genius," said Val and giggled before she asked, "So, do you like being a woman?"

"It's so exciting to be in this body, and even my mind seems to work a little differently now. Everything is new, and I feel so pretty, too," replied Tibs with a broad smile.

"You are gorgeous, Tibs."

"Thanks, you are, too, Val."

"How did you transfer so quickly, and where did you go to?"

"I never went anywhere. I used our chamber as the sender and the receiver, but it still took six hours. I had to get up early this morning. By the way, we are also immortal and forever young now."

"Oh, that's nice," said Val and snickered before she asked, "but more importantly, is it possible that I could become a man?"

"Yes, it's possible. We could roleplay in the reverse."

"Wow, our sex life will be off the charts!" exclaimed Val joyfully.

"Yeah, but we have to decide which one of us will get pregnant," noted Tiberius nonchalantly.

Val was laughing so hard she had tears in her eyes, and Tibs loved that she was so happy. After she calmed down a little, she kissed him deeply and played with Tibs' long, dark hair.

"You removed an obstacle that I never thought we could conquer in our relationship," she said softly.

"Someone very wise once told me that 'give and take' is how a relationship should work," he said with a sly smile before adding more seriously," You gave, and I took. Now I give, and you take, and hopefully, it works."

"It works, and I will prove it to you when you are a man again," she said and added, "You are truly a genius, Tibs."

Tiberius chuckled at that but didn't like the flattery. Val got out of bed and disappeared for a moment. He thought that she might be using the restroom, but a minute later, she came back with a large picture frame in her hands. It was covered with linen, and she hesitated to reveal it.

"I made this for your birthday, but I want you to have it right now," said Val, and removed the cloth.

The picture showed a black widow and a scorpion facing off under the moonlight. The painting was excellent, and Tibs had no idea that she was such a talented artist. Tiberius loved the present and was deeply moved.

"I haven't said this to anyone in my entire life, but I will say it now: I love you, Val."

"And I love you so very, very much," replied Valkyrie, then quickly put the painting down and jumped back into bed.

# 32. Betrayal

Early the next day, Valkyrie was programming the transfer chamber. It started with a hum, and the lights on the console of the machine flashed red. They would continue to flash for the next 6 hours because this was not an ordinary transfer. Val was satisfied and left the room, going outside the complex. It was a lovely day, as most were on this planet. She fetched a spade from the shed that Tiberius had built when he first arrived on this world. She picked a spot near the tomatoes and started digging. It took her several hours to enlarge the excavation, but the exercise was invigorating and cleared her mind. When it was done, she dragged the female body outside and dumped the corpse unceremoniously into the open grave. It took her another hour to refill the hole. It would have been easier to disintegrate the carcass, but Valkyrie didn't want to take chances with the alien technology. Sometimes, the old-fashioned ways were still the best. When it was finished, she looked at the grave and briefly considered adding a marker, but that would be a sentimental waste.

Tiberius had been a tough nut to crack. It had required all her skill and patience to wear him down. Smart and skeptical as he was, his downfall had been his innate desire to trust someone. She had enjoyed the battle, but in the end, Tiberius folded spectacularly and in the most ridiculous fashion. Not only had he made himself easier to kill by becoming a woman, but he also provided her with the knowledge and the means to make the perfect companion for herself.

"You can't fix stupid," she mumbled to herself and grinned.

When she returned inside, the alien program on her tablet indicated that the transfer was nearly complete. Val was excited and ran to the room with the chamber. The lights had gone blue, and she opened the lid of the pod. The woman inside was still asleep, but she was perfect: about 25 years old, tall with long legs, blue eyes, long wavy black hair, soft facial features, a shapely figure, perfect teeth, and lush lips.

"Hi, Veronica!" said Val happily as her duplicate woke up.

"What's going on?" replied the duplicate, confused to see herself.

"Welcome to your new home. I'm Valkyrie."

Veronica hesitated for a moment, but then got out of the chamber and inspected herself.

"I look perfect!" she said, gasping a little.

"Of course, just like we always imagined," said Valkyrie and softly kissed her duplicate.

"How did you do that, and how did you make two of us?"

"It's a long story, but we have lots of time for that later."

"I can't wait to hear it," said Veronica, and asked, "Is Walter gone?"

"His real name was Tiberius, but he won't be bothering us anymore," said Val, and asked, "Shall we have some champagne?"


Tiberius woke up and pushed the lid of the chamber open. He climbed out and inspected himself. He was a young and healthy man. The failsafe had worked. He didn't know exactly what had happened, but the fact that he was a man again and here on Earth meant that Valkyrie had finally killed him.

He looked around the cabin. He used to come here every summer for a few weeks. It was tranquil up here and the perfect place to do his writing. But the alien transfer chamber filled up most of the room now, and he could barely squeeze by to check out the rest of the little building. He was concerned that someone might have burglarized it since his last visit two years ago, but everything was untouched and in perfect order. He retrieved his fishing clothes from the closet and put them on. Then he rummaged through a wooden trunk and recovered his old laptop. Of course, it was out of power after being off for so long, and he would have to recharge it with the generator before it would work again. He went outside. It was a pleasant day in the Sierra Mountains, and he took a deep breath and enjoyed the fresh air. Then he went to the shed behind the cabin and started the generator. To his surprise, it still worked flawlessly after all this time.

Tiberius had some water and canned food while the laptop recharged. Of course, the computer didn't have the alien software installed; it had only an older version of Windows. However, that wasn't a problem anymore, since he had configured the controls of this particular transfer chamber to interface with any regular computer. Once that was hooked up and installed, he checked on the colony. Valkyrie had duplicated someone and modified that person to match her ideal lover. His first guess was that it must have been Megan, but then he realized that she had altered her own profile instead.

"Narcissism at its finest," he said to himself and smirked.

On a hunch, he checked the complex in Antarctica next, and it was gone. Valkyrie had settled the score with Megan as well. Tiberius was tempted to reset the building on the new planet to exact revenge on Val, but decided against it. There was a more effective and amusing way to get retribution. First, he locked down all the alien technology, and then he sent Val a short message to her tablet.

"Congratulations, little spider! Well done! Enjoy your duplicate and the great outdoors."

Only a few moments later, he got a reply and laughed out loud.

"Fuck you, Tibs!"

# 33. Honesty

About a month later, Tiberius was still at the cabin because he didn't have any other place to stay. Emotionally, he had moved on from Megan, Sylvie, and even Valkyrie. What happened on those distant worlds wasn't forgotten but had been filed away as just another, albeit fascinating, chapter of his life.

But the aliens still occupied his mind. Tiberius found that they were beetle-like creatures with six limbs and long, faceted eye stalks, similar to snails, but their bodies resembled those of mammals. They lived in large colonies or hives underground and ventured outdoors only at night. He discovered the reason why they had gone extinct, and the transfer chamber was to blame. The aliens had refined their genetic makeup to perfection into six distinct genetic profiles. Billions of aliens were duplicated from those six variations, and that had been their downfall. Without sufficient variability, a disease decimated them so quickly that they could not react in time. The alien empire was eradicated in a matter of weeks despite possessing incredible technological abilities. If the aliens could not handle it, the results would be the same, or worse, if this technology ever fell into human hands.

Tiberius kept himself busy with his writings, but admittedly, he missed the excitement and intellectual stimulation that Valkyrie had provided. One day, when he was writing, the alien program pinged him with a new message. With everyone dead, the only person who could be messaging him was Val or perhaps her duplicate. He opened the chat client.

"Tibs?"

Tiberius considered a video call but quickly discarded that idea. He didn't really want to see Val, and she shouldn't get a glimpse of his current location. So, he continued to use the text-based chat program.

"Yes?"

"I got rid of my duplicate."

"Why would you do that? She must have been perfect for you."

"She was a bitch."

"How did you dispose of her?"

"After you kicked us out, we had to explore the surroundings. There is a tar pit near that lake. Veronica slipped and fell in," typed Val, and added a moment later, "I'm sorry I killed you."

"I'm laughing so hard right now," he typed and added some laughing emojis.

"I deserve that. I'm a bitch, too."

"That's a very polite way of saying it. What do you want, Val?"

"You."

"Oh, come on!"

"I'm serious. I miss you terribly. If you didn't resurrect yourself, I would have done it by now."

Tiberius actually believed that she would have resurrected him. She had killed him, and if she had allowed him to live again, that would have established her superiority and made her victory even sweeter.

"That's not going to happen, and you know it."

"I know. Can you reset the complex?"

"Why?"

"I'm inside and want to die."

Tiberius checked the complex. The aliens had their own surveillance technology, and it confirmed that Valkyrie was currently in her old room.

"Val, if you want to die, do it yourself. There is some rope in the shed."

"Bye, Tibs."

"Wait!" he typed quickly.

"Yes?"

"I miss you, too."

She replied with only a smiley face and a heart.

"Don't kill yourself, but I can never trust you again."

"I know that, and you shouldn't trust me. I figured out your weakness. You desperately wanted to find someone you could trust. I exploited that and pretended to be that person. You resisted for a long time, but eventually, you trusted me completely and told me that you loved me. That's when I killed you in the ultimate act of betrayal. I did it to prove that I won the game. Nothing else mattered to me. I'm dangerous and deranged."

"That was probably the first honest thing you said since we've met."

"I thought you were weak because you fell for my performance, but I fell for my act, too. Everything I said was a lie, but when you were gone, my lies turned into truths. I rehashed all our conversations in my mind, and the emotions I had pretended to feel for you suddenly became real. It is the worst punishment."

"The first rule of deception: don't believe your own hubris."

"Yes, I thought I was just acting, but somewhere down the line, the bullshit wasn't bullshit anymore."

"It is understandable. When you immerse yourself in a role for as long and as deeply as you have done, the boundaries between the act and your true self become blurry."

"I betrayed you in the worst way and expected to be killed permanently, yet here you are, comforting me again. When I begged you to let me stay, you said it didn't suit me to be so submissive. Now, it doesn't suit you to be so forgiving."

"Val, I'm having fun with my dirty girl over here, so I don't really care all that much…"

"You duplicated Sylvie?!?" Veronica added a row of skull and curse emojis.

"The woman I loved killed me, so I needed a substitute. Sylvie is quite amazing."

"Kill her and come back. I'll be your dirty girl!"

"How dirty?"

"Anything you like, and some stuff you can't even imagine. I'll make Sylvie look like an amateur."

"Until you kill me again?"

"Yeah, maybe. But obviously, you'll just resurrect yourself."

"Be honest, Val. You just want a rematch."

"Best two out of three?"

He just responded with a laughing emoji, but he was pretty sure that a rematch was all that Val was really after. It was evident that she was bored out of her mind, not remorseful.

"No, Tibs, I really miss you so much. I understand now why you didn't kill Megan. Being alive and having to face your failures every moment of your existence is much worse than death."

"Sometimes a lesson must be taught, but death is a poor teacher."

"You are scary and cruel."

"Says the serial killer."

Val only responded with an evil smiley face and several coffin emojis, and Tibs had to laugh.

"Fine, you can use the complex, and I won't reset it. I will power it up again and activate the alien tech, but not the transfer chamber."

"Thanks, but I don't care. I just want you. I want our old life back. I want to dance again. I want to have breakfast with you. I want to laugh and make you laugh. It was perfect, but I threw it away because I'm insane."

"Yes, it was very nice, even if it was just an illusion."

"I lied to you, but also didn't. I'm fucked up in the head, but I love you."

"I would really have to lock you up, and I don't want to do that. Not to mention, we would still have our very real problem with the sexual preferences."

"You transformed into my ideal lover. I made my duplicate like her, too. Guess which one I liked better in bed?"

"Your duplicate, of course. After all, she was you."

"You are so wrong. It felt like I was masturbating."

"Oh? I didn't expect that, but it makes some sense."

"After I had told all our stories to Veronica, there was nothing left to talk about. What do you say to yourself that you don't already know? Very soon, I started to miss you, but Veronica mocked me for that because she never knew what we had," typed Val and added after a pause, "I watched her boil in the hot tar."

"Gruesome, but in a way, I understand."

"What you did for me was unbelievable. You don't remember, but I can love you as a man or a woman now, and that's real. Of course, I silently laughed at your genius back then because I thought it was my chance to win. But instead, I lost everything. Please kill me, Tibs."

"Nope."

"Then please come back to me! Please!"

"I might stop by someday when you least expect it."

"Is that a promise?"

"No, a threat. It's my turn to kill you a few times."

"Snuff sex, then?"

"I still love your humor," typed Tiberius and added a thumbs up.

"It's a date! You kill me while we fuck. Please record it because I want to watch after you replicate me."

"I'll see you someday, Val."

"Love you, Tibs!" typed Valkyrie and added a bunch of heart emojis.

"Sure."

# 34. A Second Chance

About two weeks after that conversation, Tiberius arrived in the middle of the night. He had suppressed all the notifications of the alien software because he didn't want to be stabbed while he was still waking up in the chamber. He pushed the lid open, and everything was quiet. He reached under the transfer chamber and was glad that the secret laptop was still there. Tibs booted it up and checked the controls and the failsafe. If he died today, he would be resurrected at the cabin again.

Val was asleep in her quarters. He exited the transfer room and silently walked to her room. The door was locked, but he had overridden the mechanism and opened it carefully. Val was in bed, covered only by a thin sheet. She was sleeping on her side, and Tibs slipped under the sheet and wrapped his arm around her waist. She woke up screaming!

"Fuck you, Tibs!" she yelled out loud, and he was laughing so hard.

Then she practically flew into his arms and showered him with kisses, but she was also crying, and her tears dropped all over his face. He held her tightly as she was sobbing in his ear.

"Hi Val," he said after she had calmed down a little.

"You came back. I love you so much, Tibs," she whispered.

"Yeah, I'm a glutton for punishment."

"No, I must be punished. I'm an awful person. Please kill me right now!"

"Can I fuck you first?" he asked with a grin.

"Of course, and I will enjoy it so much. Kill me when you cum, baby."

"That's the weirdest conversation I've ever had."

"We are the weirdest couple in history, but it doesn't matter. No more lies, no games - just sex and death. I swear it!"

"You also promised that you would never hurt me. Which brings up a good question: how did you kill me?"

"Oh, you fell asleep after sex. I suffocated you with the pillow. You struggled, but weren't that strong as a woman."

"Did I like being a woman?"

"You said you were excited to be in that body because it felt new to you. I know you liked that I liked it. You were gorgeous," Val said and took her tablet from the nightstand to show him some pictures.

"Wow, sexy! Maybe I can do that again someday if you promise not to kill me."

"I would love that. Not the killing, but you as a woman. But don't use my ideal lover again. There are too many bad memories attached to it. Become your own ideal woman."

"That won't work."

"Why not?"

"Because you are my ideal woman, and then it would feel like your duplicate again."

"Thanks, but I'm far from ideal, Tibs. It's okay if you want to look like me, but you're not me. I would still love you."

"Well, maybe I'll become an exotic beauty next time," said Tibs and asked, "Was the sex good?"

"It was awesome. You were awesome! I climaxed a bunch of times."

"And then you killed me?"

"Yeah."

"And what happened after that?"

"I fucked your corpse one more time, then killed Megan, made my duplicate, and buried you by the tomatoes. I added the tombstone later. When it was done, I got drunk and had sex with my alter ego," said Val, and added with a sigh, "I'm so messed up."

"How many people have you killed back on Earth?"

"Just one," said Val and elaborated, "I went rock climbing with my girlfriend right after she cleaned out my bank account and dumped me, and just before I met Megan. I made her gear malfunction, and she went splat. It was in the news, but the investigation blamed it on the company that had rented us the stuff. I even got some money out of it, which I used later to stock this place with supplies."

"Val, before we do anything. I want you to come with me to the transfer chamber."

"OK, but why?"

"It won't hurt, but we need to scan you. It will update your personality information to the current state."

"Oh, I see. My duplicate was the Veronica that arrived after she had destroyed the old colony."

"Correct, that's the latest profile, but we have to update it, or you won't remember what happened to us if you die."

"And I would kill you again just to win the game?"

"Most likely."

"OK, but can we do that later? I want to be your dirty girl," said Val, and pouted a little.

"No, let's do it right now, in case I really kill you tonight," said Tiberius and got out of bed.

"Tibs?" she asked as she got up too.

"Yes?"

"I'm serious. I want you to kill me, and please make it painful, too. Is that weird?"

"Meh, coming from you, it's pretty tame," he said nonchalantly and shrugged his shoulders.

Val laughed out loud and followed Tiberius to the room with the transfer chamber. Tiberius scanned her in the pod, and it took only about 10 minutes. He checked the results and was satisfied. Val climbed out of the chamber and embraced him.

"I can't believe you are really here after I murdered you in cold blood. You are as insane as I am, Tibs."

"I always was, but I'm not as violent. Tonight will be the first time I kill someone."

"Liar, you killed Sylvie's duplicate."

"Naa, I never duplicated her. I just wanted you to be my dirty girl," said Tiberius and grinned at her.

"God, I was so jealous! Well played, Tibs," replied Val and shook her head.

"Jealous of Sylvie? You are a lousy lesbian," teased Tiberius.

"I'm very possessive of my playthings if you haven't noticed," said Val, and added, "Now get on with the raping and killing, and don't forget to record everything."

What happened in the next hour was indescribable: Valkyrie unleashed the monster in him, and Tiberius lost all control over himself for the very first time in his life. He didn't fully understand how she was able to do that. For all he knew, it wasn't her betrayal or his lust that made him do unspeakable things. He indulged in the liberating rage while simultaneously being utterly sickened by it. Valkyrie suffered tremendously yet continued to ask for more and enjoyed the torment until the very end. Tiberius didn't regret what he had done, but it would never, ever happen again!

About six hours later, Val exited the chamber, embraced Tibs, and kissed him deeply.

"You really killed me," she said happily.

"You deserved it."

"I did! I hope you got it all on camera?" asked Val excitedly.

"With audio, too."

"Let me see my dead body first."

"It's still in your room, but it looks a little rough," replied Tiberius with a slight frown.

"Good, let's go," she said, took his hand, and almost dragged him behind her.

They went to Val's room and looked at the corpse on her bed. She had blood on her face, severe strangulation marks on her neck, and her spine looked broken. Val touched her and left her hand on the cold body for a moment.

"I died smiling."

"It was surreal. Your former self thanked me just before she died."

"I was grateful because you made it stop," said Val cryptically and continued more upbeat, "Thank you, Tibs. Now, please show me the recording."

Val watched the video and quickly became very aroused. He kissed her neck, and she gasped, but she remained fixated on the screen of her tablet. When the video ended, she dropped the tablet on the bed and turned around.

"I never thought death could be so sexy."

"I'm glad you are alive again, but not sorry that I killed you, if that makes any sense."

"And you shouldn't be sorry. I deserved so much worse," said Val, and added with a sigh, "What I did to you was unforgivable. I hurt you so much."

"It probably would have hurt a lot more when I was your age, but now it was just another Tuesday for me. More importantly, the pain didn't stem from the betrayal because that was always expected. What hurt was my failure to predict how and when it would happen. No matter how much I prepare, life always finds a new way to defeat me. I'm not upset with you, but disappointed in myself and thoroughly disenchanted with existence. I took that out on your former self."

"You released a lifetime of frustrations, and I'm glad you did because it needed to happen," said Val, and asked, "Why did you come back to me?"

"I'm here because I enjoyed our game and was mesmerized by your skill and patience. Like a true spider, you entangled me in invisible silk and patiently waited until I was immobilized before you moved in for that venomous bite. But you forgot about my stinger and lost in the end."

"You came to gloat?"

"Not really, since the ultimate outcome was never in question with the failsafe. But you are the one sharp needle, and it took me a lifetime to find you, so why would I abandon my favorite playmate? I came to give you what you really want – a rematch."

"Our game is a combination of chess and poker. We will set up the pieces and shuffle the deck. We are fascinated by the contest and eager to outdo one another. But the game has us trapped, and nothing between us can ever be real."

"That is true."

"Search your heart before you answer: do you want that, Tibs?"

"We have fun playing and can enjoy each other's company. People like us cannot expect much more," he said and asked, "You are right: we are trapped in the game, but how can we exit?"

"We just quit," said Val, and asked, "How do normal people do it?"

"I can't answer that."

"Yeah, me neither. I guess ordinary folks just trust each other blindly."

"I suppose so, but I don't see how that's an option for us."

"We could try."

"We could try, and I believe both of us would make a genuine effort until we slip into our old, comfortable habits of mistrust and deceit again. Whoever abandons the effort first will win the next round, and the other will hate themselves for being so naïve."

"Tibs, it's so depressing. I want to show you how much you mean to me. You are so much more than just a playmate. But I don't know how I can make you understand so that you would believe me."

"I'm in the same boat and have no solution. Whatever I say, you either won't believe it or use it against me in our contest. In all my previous relationships, it was the point when I would walk away."

"We overcame one humongous obstacle; can't we overcome this too?"

"Did we really overcome that? You are not attracted to men in general or me in particular, but you sort of make an exception or maybe just tolerate my affections a little better," said Tiberius with a shrug, and added, "Unless you have an idea, there is no solution."

"I'm still appalled by men, but you are not a man. You are my Tibs. Whatever incarnation you might choose, I will enjoy you to the fullest. But, of course, you won't believe me, since I've lied so much. Our problem is that we cannot trust each other, and rightfully so," said Val, and continued, "We must focus on one truth at a time: I like you, Tibs. Do you believe me?"

"I believe you, and I like you too, Val. Do you believe that?"

"Yes. I like being with you and all the things we did: talking, laughing, dancing, gardening, having our meals together, and watching the stars at night."

"I liked those things too, and I miss them."

"Do you believe that I have never been so close to anyone in my life?"

"I have no way to know for sure, but I suppose I have not been this close to anyone either."

"OK, we have established a foundation of truth," said Val and smiled at him before she added, "Now we have to build on that."

Tiberius considered it carefully. They liked each other and each other's company, and he was closer to Val than anyone else. He concluded that she was right about these fundamental truths. Perhaps that was enough of a foundation to rebuild their relationship?

"You are an excellent therapist, Val."

"Thanks, Tibs," said Val and continued, "Do you believe that I would die for you without resurrection?"

"You would also kill me without resurrection, and you already did that."

"I know, and I'm sorry, but please answer the question."

"I could see you killing for me, but not dying for me. That's just not you, Val."

"But I know you would die for me because you already did that."

"What do you mean?"

"You always expected that I would kill you someday, yet you let it happen. You literally and figuratively died for my pleasure."

"I didn't think of it like that."

"Nobody would do that, not even with a failsafe. Anyone else would kill first or run away. But not you," said Val and concluded, "You don't just like me; you love me."

"Hmm."

"I love you, too, Tibs. That's why I died for your pleasure today and left it up to you if you resurrect me."

"Of course, you knew that I would."

"I only knew what you showed me and hoped that it was the truth. But I want to prove to you that I trust you with my life. Please kill me again and then decide."

"Do you really want to quit the game, or have we graduated from poker to Russian Roulette?"

"I'm quitting the game, but I don't want to be without you. If I cannot be with you, I want to die and beg you to never resurrect me."

"Val, that's emotional blackmail. Don't do that because you won't like my response."

"I'm sorry, Tibs. It wasn't meant in that way."

"Yeah, I know that," said Tiberius, and suggested, "I could duplicate myself for you. Perhaps even as a woman?"

"No! I'm done with duplicates. I would just kill him or her again because I want the original."

"Do you want to return to Earth?"

"You can do that?"

"Yes. You will be young and healthy with a new identity. I will also make sure that you have a roof over your head and are financially secure."

"But I will never see you again?"

"No, since I would stay here. You won't be able to contact me because I will destroy the alien technology on Earth, including the relay. Humanity cannot be trusted with this gift."

"It's a generous offer, but I want to stay here with you," said Val, shaking her head.

Tiberius was out of suggestions. Valkyrie was unstable and dangerous, but she desperately wanted to be with him again, and he had to admit that he desired her company, too. If he stayed with her, it was a certainty that one of them would die again, but perhaps that's how it was supposed to be?

"You are such a skilled manipulator, and this is the outcome you wanted from the start. But fine, we will play Adam and Eve again."

"I'm not playing this time, remember that…," said Val, but suddenly stopped talking.

"But?" asked Tiberius, but Valkyrie looked distraught and didn't reply for a while.

"I'm not well and so afraid," said Val finally, and started crying.

"What's wrong? Why are you afraid?"

"I can't stop the thoughts!"

"What are you thinking?"

"While I was telling you how much I love you, a part of me was already plotting to deceive you again," admitted Val and exclaimed, "I can't stop it! It's always been like this since I was a little girl. Please just kill me. I will be grateful to you again."

"Come on, I've known for a long time that you are not well. I didn't care then, and it's not bothering me now."

"I told you once that you mean everything to me. I thought I was lying back then, but it was always the truth. You are my everything, but I don't deserve you. I'm so afraid that I will hurt you again."

"I'm not so different. I can't stop thinking, either. That's why I write books. You have read one and know how twisted my mind is."

"I have read all your books," she said, and continued, "Do you remember when we talked about therapy back at the old colony? I'm insane, but I know that I'm insane. It's asking a lot, but I want your help and will listen to your advice. You have to be my therapist because nobody else could do it."

"I'm not qualified," said Tibs, but added, "You see life just as entertainment and a contest. You have empathy but lack compassion. I lack that, too, but you are more deficient. If we were on Earth, I would suggest that you get a pet and learn how to take care of all its needs. I always had cats for that reason, and they kept me sane, more or less."

"I have given that advice to some of my clients but never considered it for myself," said Val, and asked with a little smile, "Will you be my pet?"

"Meow," replied Tibs, and Val giggled a little.

"But the lack of compassion is just the tip of the iceberg. I can't stop the thoughts! That's why I kept a diary since I was 8 years old. It's the most messed-up thing you can imagine. My mind is constantly racing, day and night, and I'm drowning. I wake up at odd hours to write things down, and it's all crazy, deranged shit. It's my most private and most shameful possession, but you must read it. Your mind is different, too, so maybe you can understand?"

Valkyrie was pleading insanity now, possibly to appeal to his sympathy or maybe to his intellectual prowess, so that he would try to fix her problem. Considering how gifted an actress she was, those were distinct possibilities. But perhaps she was truthful for once, and Tiberius tended to believe that because she was willing to provide proof in the form of her diary. He resolved to give her the benefit of the doubt for now.

"I will read it."

"Thanks, but it will be awful. Some things in there are about you, and they are not kind."

"What exactly happens in your mind?"

"I'm not schizophrenic. I don't hear voices or see things that are not there. I also don't have multiple personality disorder. I just can't stop the thoughts."

"Can you describe it?"

"Let's say we have breakfast. We are joking around and discussing what we will do that day. I'm relaxed and happy to be with you. Suddenly and without warning, between a bite of toast and a sip of coffee, a terrible thought pops into my mind, suggesting that I should make breakfast next time, so I have a chance to poison you."

"To the outside, nothing has changed: I'm still smiling, drinking coffee, and chatting with you. But now my mind is racing - which poison should I use, where can I get it, how will I administer it, and so on. A part of me is screaming to stop these awful thoughts, but I'm not in charge anymore."

"You are dripping," said Tiberius, seemingly unrelated, and Val looked confused but then inspected herself and noticed that her breasts were lactating vigorously.

"What did you do to me?" she wondered, looking at him.

"You are not pregnant, don't worry."

"It's kinky. Is that a fantasy of yours?"

"It's inspiring, but it wasn't a fetish," said Tiberius and explained, "Val, you have to learn how to be nurturing, and I have to learn how to trust you again. It will be a very slow process for both of us, but nature provides."

Valkyrie realized immediately what he meant. She seemed surprised but considered the idea for a moment. Then she smiled broadly at him and nodded.

"Oh my, you are truly a genius. I cannot say this often enough."

"Don't do that if you are serious about stopping our competition."

"Do what?"

"Criticize me if you must, and I'll consider that to be honest. But if you praise me, I know that you are playing again."

"You cannot take a compliment even if it's genuine because you believe it's manipulation?"

"Manipulation is the sole purpose of any compliment, Val."

"Explain that, please," said Val with a curious look on her face.

"For example, if I compliment you on your kindness, it becomes less likely that you will be cruel to me. If I praise your loyalty, you will be less inclined to betray me, and so on. For better or worse, every compliment comes with an agenda."

"You have a point, Tibs. But genius or not, your idea might still work," replied Val, and smiled at him.

Then she gently pushed him down on the edge of the bed and sat on his lap with her legs folded behind his back. She adjusted herself so he could enter her. Val supported one breast with the palm of her hand and leaned forward a little to bring it closer to his lips. He licked a drop of milk from her nipple, paused for a moment, and smiled at her. She kissed his head fondly. Then he started to suckle while she was slowly grinding her hips. It was an unprecedented experience for Valkyrie, and perhaps for the first time in her life, her mind suddenly stopped in the moment. She had found a tiny sliver of peace, and it felt so good.

"We will do this every day, maybe many times a day," she whispered after a while.

"Yes, we will," replied Tibs and continued to feed.

"Someday, when I'm better, I can be your Eve, or you can be mine. We will live in paradise with our children, no longer trapped in a stupid contest," said Val softly, and started to hum a lullaby.

The game was afoot again.

# 35. True Colors

They lived in nearly perfect harmony for the following year, and Val continued to show steady improvement. Tibs was pleased to see her progress, and she seemed happy as well. But Tiberius knew that it could change in the blink of an eye, and for that reason, he backed up his personality every morning after he got up. The procedure only took a few minutes, wasn't uncomfortable, and felt like a short nap. Val didn't know about it, and by the time she appeared for breakfast, the update had already finished.

Tiberius woke up in the chamber. He remained there for a moment before opening the lid. He felt like he had slept for a very long time. He touched his face, and it was still cleanly shaven, but Tiberius feared that Val had done it again. He opened the lid and was almost surprised that he was still on the planet, not at the cabin on Earth. He got out and removed the laptop that was stashed underneath the pod. It was dead. He checked the controls of the transfer chamber. The device was in standby mode, not fully active, and the readouts were unusual. The aliens had a different way of keeping time, but Tiberius estimated that he must have been in that chamber for several years.

Valkyrie had not killed him this time. She must have figured out what he was doing in the mornings and had patiently waited until the procedure had become a habit for him. When she was certain that he didn't check the parameters thoroughly anymore, she put him in suspended animation so that he couldn't resurrect himself again. That was cunning and effective. But she couldn't have known, and he didn't either, that the transfer chamber would undergo automated maintenance and reanimate him during that process.

Tiberius left the room with the chamber and checked out the complex. It had been abandoned for years. He opened the big iris that served as the front door. It was daytime, and he saw that their garden had died, and even the shed was in poor shape. Tiberius went back inside. The laptop's battery was dead and wouldn't recharge, but the machine still started up when connected to the complex's power grid. It confirmed his suspicions: he had been unconscious for almost ten years. Val had left about one hour before he performed his routine personality backup. She had modified the program's parameters very subtly. He hadn't checked thoroughly and put himself into stasis indefinitely.

Val must have learned a lot about the alien software, much more than he had suspected. She had created another transfer chamber on Earth, and that's where she went. However, about six years later, she attempted to return here, but the transfer chamber was occupied by him, and the machine could not recreate her. Val had been stuck in the queue for the last four years. He laughed out loud – so clever, yet so foolish!

He studied the logs carefully. Val's new transfer chamber on Earth was completely inactive. Even the one in the cabin didn't respond appropriately. In fact, the whole ball of Play-Doh didn't execute his commands as it should. Something catastrophic must have occurred on Earth. He pinged the relay in Earth's orbit and almost immediately realized what had happened. Earth was in a nuclear winter. Humanity had finally destroyed itself, and Valkyrie had barely escaped annihilation. He sat down and contemplated his options. Eventually, he reached a decision, and for the next few days, Tiberius was busy building another complex. When it was finished, he was going to send Val's metadata to that transfer chamber, but then decided to recreate her here first. However, she was too dangerous to be fully restored, so he changed her profile to omit her arms and legs. Six hours later, the transfer chamber had created her head and torso. Tiberius opened the lid when she had awakened.

"Hello, Veronica," he said, addressing her by her proper name.

"Damn!" she yelled when she saw him.

"Why do you hate me so much?" asked Tiberius, looking at her expectantly.

"Because you are just like him!" she replied loudly.

"Like whom?"

"My swine of a father, who raped me when I was 8 years old."

"I'm very sorry to hear that," replied Tiberius, and sighed.

Finally, he had learned the sad truth. Tiberius had read her diaries, and they were as disturbing as she had claimed. He suspected that something terrible must have happened in her youth, but she had never documented it. Veronica was the victim of a horrendous betrayal, and that's why she couldn't help doing it to him. It had warped her emotions and driven her to insanity.

"You raped me, too, countless times."

"It was never forced or coerced. Either you offered, or I asked, and you consented whenever I've touched you."

"So what? I told you that I hated men, and you still did it."

"It wasn't fear, gratitude, or pity when you offered sex after I allowed you to stay here. It was a test."

"Yes, and you failed like all men do."

"I failed, and every time we were intimate, it reinforced your hatred. You were always going to destroy me, weren't you?"

"Of course! You should have stayed dead the first time. When you messaged me to gloat, I had to do it again."

Tiberius was not going to argue with her irrationality. This was one battle he could never win, and he didn't want to win it either. For the first time since they had met, she revealed her true nature, and it was surreal: Veronica had seduced him so she could despise him when he finally succumbed to her advances. He felt sorry for her, but that was not going to change his mind. This time, her actions would have serious consequences.

"This was all about getting even with your dad?"

"No, not all."

"Winning then?"

"You are arrogant and condescending. I had to prove that I was better than you."

"True, and yet you failed again," he replied with a sigh.

"Fuck you!" spat Veronica and asked snidely, "I have no arms and legs, so you can violate me more easily?"

"No, it was just a safety precaution. You will be fully restored after your next transfer."

"Earth is gone. Where are you sending me?" she asked, and Tiberius noticed the concern in her voice.

"To a familiar place with like-minded people whom you already know."

"No…," she replied, suspecting what he had planned.

"Yes, I have restored the original colony. Megan and all your friends are there, even Mark," said Tiberius, but didn't mention that Ron, the only actual victim, wouldn't be resurrected out of mercy.

"NO!!!" she shouted, and he could see the desperation in her eyes.

"But this time, it's a one-way street. No more games, no more transfers, just you and the other savages. I even improved your genetics. If you don't kill each other, you will live at least 300 years," said Tiberius with a thin smile.

"No, please! Not that! Kill me instead and purge my profile! Please! PLEASE!" she begged, and tears were running down her cheeks.

"Oh, you know that I don't like to kill anyone since death is such a poor teacher," said Tiberius calmly and added as he closed the lid, "Goodbye, little spider."

Tiberius didn't mention the most amusing twist because that should remain a surprise for Veronica and the other colonists. When they killed each other, and Tiberius was sure that they would, the alien device would recreate them over and over. He initiated the transfer and then went to the kitchen to make some fresh coffee.

One month later, Tiberius found a handwritten note in Val's old room while he was cleaning up:

*If you find this message, I have betrayed you again and have lost once more, but I'm relieved. We were both deceived as children. I don't know what happened to you, but I was abused by my father. You made yourself immune to betrayal, while I chose to become the betrayer. I cannot tell right from wrong or lies from the truth, but I know that you are my everything, Tibs – my infinite love and my undying hatred. Our time was precious to me since you stopped the thoughts for a little while. However, they always came back stronger, but I fought them for as long and as hard as I could. Do not forgive me, and do not give me another chance because I will betray you again and again. I cannot stop it because I'm insane, but I love you – always have and always will. Val.*

# 36. Redemption

It's been six months since he banished Veronica. Tiberius kept himself busy studying the aliens. He discovered even more of their secrets and was now able to read their language as well. He wrote an entire book on their technology and culture. It was a fascinating topic, and there were many lessons to be learned from both their achievements and their demise.

Tiberius also checked on Earth a few times and even repaired the transfer chamber at the cabin. But Earth was desolate, and it depressed him to look at it with the alien relay. Hundreds of millions had died in the nuclear holocaust, but there were still billions of people living on the planet. But their numbers were dwindling rapidly now: sure, the richest of the rich lived comfortably in underground bunkers, island enclaves, or had traveled to outer space, but the rest of humanity suffered immeasurably. Radioactive fallout covered the entire planet, causing widespread cancer and grotesque mutations, and the nuclear winter made the crops fail, resulting in a lasting global famine. Natural disasters of every type struck unmitigated, and without any healthcare, old and new diseases exacted a horrific toll. The few governments that still existed were fascist or theocratic, brutally oppressing and exploiting their vanishing slice of humanity. Homo sapiens had reverted to its most savage nature, and there was no turning back. The internet and all its information were gone, and physical books were more often used to start a fire than to be read. Worse yet, an entire generation was growing up illiterate and unenlightened because there was nobody left to teach them how to read, how to think critically, and what it meant to be sapient.

Tiberius's home country was particularly forbidding. Even when he was still on Earth, decency and civility had been eroding steadily, and ignorance, prejudice, and greed had held the nation in a tight grip. But now the violence and cruelty had reached unprecedented heights. It was a Wild West-style anarchy, but with vehicles and automatic weapons, where kindness was considered weakness, and only might made right. Once a beacon of freedom and tolerance, the former United States of America, or what little was left of it, had become the complete opposite, and it weighed heavily on Tiberius' heart and mind.

Despite keeping himself occupied on the alien planet with various tasks, Tiberius agonized many times over whether he should reach out to Veronica again. Rationally, he knew that he shouldn't, but emotionally, he missed her sorely. One day, just after breakfast, when Tiberius was looking at the marvelous painting of the spider and the scorpion, he activated Veronica's tablet and sent her a message.

*When you killed me the first time, I was surprised. When you let me rot in the transfer chamber, I was disappointed, annoyed, and frustrated, but I wasn't hurt. But when we last spoke, you said that I was like him. I'm not your father, and I never want to be like him! It hurt so much, and it still does. That's why I punished you the way I did.*

He didn't have to wait long for an answer. Only a few minutes later, Veronica's response arrived.

*I was on Earth for 6 years. I had grand plans to rule the damn planet with the alien tech. But do you know what I really did? I got drunk and high and partied my ass off the entire time because whenever I was sober, I missed you so much, and the guilt was killing me. I was a wreck and ready to die when Earth went to hell, but I wanted to see you one last time. But when I did, all I saw was my father. My insane hatred ruled me again when I said those words to you. You are not him, and I know that. But you are as tall as he was, as bright and strong as he was. You are just as condescending, and you even resemble him a little. My dad meant everything to me, and betrayed everything. Ever since we've met, I still see his face whenever I look at you.*

Tiberius was still reading when another message arrived.

*Will you tell me how you became so messed up?*

He was happy that Veronica had replied, but unsure how to answer her question.

*I never talked to you about my past because there was no single traumatic event. I became who I am because of a thousand little cuts. I absorbed the lessons, controlled my emotions, and adjusted my behavior. I keenly observed the world and learned as much as I could. I became entirely self-sufficient and was prepared for all eventualities, but it isolated me from everyone else. I was lonely at first, but then I accepted it and finally came to like it that way. But then you happened.*

Tiberius waited for half an hour, but Veronica didn't answer. Just when he was about to close the messaging program, the software pinged with her reply.

*My parents were happily married. They were affluent and had promising careers. It all changed when I was born. My mother became abusive and violent, and the marriage finally failed when I was seven. I wanted to stay with my dad because he was always kind to me. But my mother got custody, and I could only see him twice a month. My mom started drinking and had a new boyfriend every few weeks. My dad became depressed and reclusive. He didn't want to see anyone aside from me. By age ten, my father was dead, and my mother had moved to South America, leaving me with my grandparents. I never talked to her again. My grandparents took care of me, raised me well, and ensured I received a good education and a solid start. I learned how to fit in, but the damage was done. My mind was a mess, and it only got worse with every passing year.*

Tiberius switched on the text chat.

"Did you kill your father?"

"No. I wanted to kill him, but I was still little when he died in a car accident. I was so happy when it happened, but then I missed him so much, and the paradox scrambled my brain."

Tiberius didn't respond. He searched his mind and heart for a long time before he discovered the undeniable truth: for him, there was nobody else in the universe like Valkyrie. She was ill and dangerous, but he needed her back.

"I know you will try to kill me again, but I'd rather be dead than without you, Val."

"I'd rather suffer here for all eternity than hurt you again, Tibs."

"You don't want to see me?" typed Tiberius.

"Of course, I do! But I cannot be cured, I cannot be trusted, and I will hurt you."

186

"I cannot heal you, but perhaps the aliens can."

"What do you mean?"

"The transfer chamber can change the physical appearance, but could also edit the mind."

"You want to change my personality?"

"It's a whole new level of violation beyond rape, and I won't change anything without your explicit consent. But I could remove or lessen some traumatic memories."

"Like my father raping me every other weekend for two years until he died?"

"My goodness, I'm so sorry, Val!" typed Tiberius, utterly appalled by that piece of information.

"It's OK," replied Val after a long pause.

"Yes, I could do that or at least lessen the pain and smooth over the scars."

"I would still remember it, but it wouldn't hurt as badly, and perhaps I wouldn't want to kill you anymore?"

"Maybe, but I don't know for sure if it works. I would create a backup first, and if it fails, I would restore your old self."

"Mind control, or therapy Vulcan style?" typed Val and added the Vulcan salute emoji.

"I still love your humor. It's risky, and you would have to trust me like you have never trusted anyone before."

"I'm the betrayer, not you. Do it, Tibs!"

"Are you sure?"

"I'm sure. I don't want to be like this. A part of me is already plotting again, eager to get another shot at you. Tibs, if this doesn't work, and you have even the slightest doubt, send me back here immediately."

"Understood. Please go to your transfer chamber, enter the pod, and I'll do the rest."

"I can't. You have created hell."

"What do you mean?"

"The colony has gone mad; they are raping and killing each other almost daily. I have died a couple of times already and killed probably everyone here at least once. It started when Kevin tried to murder Mark out of jealousy. Now we have factions: Kevin, Lillian, Jaques, Ahmed, and Juan are one. Megan, Mark, Yue, and Irina are the other."

"Do you have a faction?"

"Sort of," replied Val cryptically.

Tiberius checked the alien surveillance. It indicated that another person was in Valkyrie's room, resting on the bed, but he couldn't tell who it was because the program didn't include visuals.

"I noticed that there is someone else in your room."

"Our little dirty girl is here, and now I know why you call her that. She is my faction. Should I kill her? She will be resurrected anyway."

"I don't think that will get you to the transfer chamber."

"No, it won't. Ahmed is guarding that room with an axe, and Mark is patrolling out there with some kind of crossbow. Sylvie and I are neutral, but that doesn't mean much here."

Tiberius didn't respond for a moment. He made some quick adjustments to the structure, specifically Val's quarters.

"I see. Your room is now sealed off, and nobody can get in. Take Sylvie to your bathroom and stay there. We'll decide what to do with her after I have spawned a transfer chamber in your quarters."

"You can do that?"

"Yes, and if the mind edit works, I will teach you everything I know someday."

"I don't think I should know everything even if I'm cured."

Val waited in the bathroom and watched as a transfer chamber slowly rose from the floor of her room. Sylvie was excited and wanted to know what was happening. Instead of answering her questions, Val kissed her deeply and then jammed a knife into her stomach. Sylvie died moments later while Tibs was still running some tests. The lights on the console flashed in different colors for a few minutes, but then they all turned blue.

"OK, it's ready. Last chance to back out, Val?" typed Tiberius, but Valkyrie was already inside the pod.

"Sylvie is dead. Do it, Tibs!" she replied with a thumbs-up emoji.

Tiberius didn't want to kill Sylvie, but perhaps that was the cleanest solution. He disabled Sylvie's regeneration. Soon, he would have to make changes to the whole colony. It had gotten out of hand.

"Alright, you are coming home."

"Home - I like that," typed Val, added a heart emoji, and then closed the lid of the pod.

# 37. Adam and Eve

Tiberius left Valkyrie in the buffer for several days. Editing her mind was delicate work and not very intuitive. The alien program displayed wave patterns on a time axis according to the age of the memory, while the amplitude indicated the strength or activity of that recollection. It took him two days to identify and isolate the memories related to her father and those pertaining to him. Tiberius worked slowly and diligently because any mistake could alter Val's personality in unexpected ways. Finally, he applied the changes to her profile, initiated the creation process, and hoped for the best. Six hours later, Val woke up.

"Tibs!" she squealed as she jumped out of the pod.

"Hey Val," he replied with a big smile.

"God, I missed you so much," Val said, and she embraced him.

"I missed you, too, little spider," said Tiberius and added, "I was going to welcome you as an exotic beauty, but I wanted to see how you react to me as a man."

She nodded and let go of the embrace. She looked at Tibs seriously for several minutes, assessing her thoughts and feelings.

"I have all my terrible memories, but I feel differently about them now. Disappointment and sadness, but not rage or vengeance, and the pain is subtle, not crippling."

"Do you still compare me to your father?"

"No! I cannot believe I ever did. I'm so sorry, Tibs."

"It's fine. Are the thoughts still there?"

"My mind is quiet, and I don't want to kill you."

"That's progress."

"At least not more than usual," said Val with a smirk, but added quickly, "I'm joking! I feel good, really good. Almost as good as when you were suckling. We will do that again, right?"

"Anything you like. Anything, Val," said Tibs and kissed her forehead.

"You said you were going to welcome me as a woman. Why didn't you change my sexuality?"

"You didn't consent to that, and I like you the way you are."

"You stuck with the lesbian psycho? You are too damn noble. Now we have to go through all of that again…"

"Oh, we do?" asked Tiberius, visibly disappointed.

She looked at him, sighed deeply, and shook her head. Tiberius feared that something had gone wrong with the edit, but after a moment, Val just grinned and poked him in the belly:

"No, silly!"

"Welcome home, Val," replied Tiberius, and laughed out loud.

"I'm so happy to be home," said Val softly before she quipped, "You have been without a woman for 10 years and still don't have a goat. I know you are dying to have sex, so let's do it already. But from next week on, we'll take turns with the genders."

Tiberius was delighted because he had missed Val's racy humor so much. But he knew that she was right, too: he craved intimacy and would enjoy her to the fullest. He wanted to go to her room, but Val didn't give him a chance. She pulled him into the transfer chamber. The pod was cramped with two people inside, but they didn't care. They made love hard and fast, and Tiberius was out of breath when they had finished.

"Thank you, Val."

"Oh, don't thank me for something that I enjoyed just as much."

"No girl, thanks for being here again!" stated Tibs loudly and laughed before he added, "But the sex was nice too."

The transfer chamber became indispensable to their lives in the next few weeks. Tiberius explained all the functions to Valkyrie, and she was a swift learner. As a surprise, she transferred a pair of kittens from Earth, and Tiberius was delighted. He loved cats, and Val did, too, even though she had never had them before. They named the furry bundles Sasha and Misha, and the kittens quickly became the center of their attention. Valkyrie doted over the little rascals like a mother, and Tiberius found that heartwarming but also reassuring that Val's personality had changed for the better.

Val genuinely enjoyed intimacy with Tiberius now, but she still preferred women, and the alien device proved critical in clearing the hurdle of their sexual alignments. The options were nearly limitless, and Tibs and Val used the machine frequently to give each other erotic surprises. At one point, Val even changed into Sylvie and played the role of the dirty girl for him, but then Tibs got a playful revenge when he became Megan for her. Thanks to the transfer chamber, their sex life was vigorous, delightful, and fulfilling.

"What happened to us? You are a horny teenager, and I'm a bitch in heat," said Val and giggled.

"Yeah, but it's not just lust. I've never been so close to someone, and it almost hurts," replied Tibs as he was playing with the kittens.

"I know, Tibs. I want to feel you all the time. It's nearly an obsession," she said, but then added in a business-like voice, "We were emotionally deprived as children. Now, we have found someone like us, and it is quite natural that we are trying to make up for that deficiency. We have become codependent on each other."

"I concur with that astute assessment, Dr. Parsons," said Tiberius formally, and Val smirked.

"When I was on Earth and not puking my guts out from the booze and drugs, I researched everything I could find on you. I studied your family history, identified the places where you've lived, learned, and worked, and I've read all your scientific publications. I even know that your first cat was called Boots. Then I searched the long list of your former girlfriends and found out that I wasn't the first crazy chick who tried to kill you. The long scar on your left shoulder was not an accident but a botched knife attack. Someday, when you are ready, I want to hear about that," said Valkyrie and concluded, "You were always on my mind, Tiberius von Rittenburg."

"You were thorough. Sandra was not like you, but she was troubled, too. I was well-to-do at the time, and we were together for five years. We didn't have sex often and took precautions, but she still got pregnant. She called it a miracle baby and decided to keep it. I approved and was going to marry her, but I insisted on a paternity test. She accused me of being mistrusting, and we argued many times. One day, when it dawned on her that I would not budge, she flew into a rage, grabbed the sharpest kitchen knife, and tried to stab my chest. I evaded, but she sliced up my left shoulder. I was seriously injured but didn't go to the hospital to avoid the legal implications for her sake. Instead, I stitched it up myself and probably didn't do the best job, so it left a large scar. The next day, they found her dead in a motel. Sandra had overdosed on alcohol and painkillers. The subsequent autopsy determined that the unborn child wasn't mine. The scar has been a constant reminder ever since, but I'm glad it's gone now," said Tibs, and sighed.

"I'm sorry, Tibs," said Val and held onto his hand.

"I was in my thirties when it happened. By that time, I had already learned most of life's important lessons. It hurt, but it was not traumatic."

"Just one of the thousand cuts," said Val and nodded before she added softly, "She was another betrayer, but I'm not surprised that the broken ones are drawn to you."

"Yes, but I'm drawn to them too because they are different," admitted Tiberius, adding with a little smile, "You love my company, and I love yours."

"Those were my words, and even back then, they weren't a lie," said Val with a sigh and asked, "How do you feel about Earth?"

"People worked their jobs, had their families, and adhered to societal norms without ever questioning anything. Then they raised their children the same way, and by the same dubious values. But god, nature, or the universe gave humanity the gift of sapience and critical thought. Instead of using it for the better, most ignored it altogether, or even counteracted it and reverted to animals," said Tiberius and paused for a moment before he continued, "No, much worse than animals: they never stopped lying, worshipped greed, and indulged in vanity, prejudice, complacency, and willful ignorance. Predictably, that destroyed them in the end."

"They called people like us insane, but in reality, we were the buoyed ones in an ocean of drowning lunatics."

"Ironic, but probably true," replied Tiberius, adding with a smile, "I love your metaphors."

"I feel sad for the few who knew better and tried to be better, but the savage, vast majority deserved extinction. Humans had their chance and blew it," said Val, but added more cheerfully, "We are going down a very dark rabbit hole. Let's go outside and tend to the garden. The kittens want to play, and I need some fresh air."

Tiberius had left the garden barren, but Valkyrie was adamant about restoring it. She liked fresh fruits and veggies, but also saw it as a new beginning, and he agreed with her. It took a few weeks, but the allotment was thriving again, with tomatoes, blueberry plants, carrots, lettuce, and even a small apple tree. Val had also planted some indigenous wildflowers on Tiberius' grave. He thought that was a little morbid, considering that he was alive again, but Val insisted on that symbolic gesture. Now, they were walking among the newly planted produce, checking if the seeds had sprouted, while Sasha and Misha were pouncing on each other.

"Do you feel strange when you are a woman?" asked Valkyrie as she pulled a weed from the strawberry patch.

"It's new and different, but also exciting. Do you like being a man?"

"It's the same for me: new, different, and exciting," said Val, and added, "I know you hate compliments, but your taste in women is exquisite. Every single incarnation has been so beautiful and inspiring."

"I take that compliment, and I'm happy that you like my looks," said Tiberius, and smiled.

"Most men would never do what you do for me."

"Too many men think that they are not masculine unless they are aggressive, domineering, and abusive because society tells them that's what a real man should be like. Jacques was that type, and I disliked him greatly. There is nothing manly about these so-called high-T alpha males. They are just pussy-grabbing swine in my book."

"I couldn't have said it better myself," said Val and joked, "you would make a good bull dyke."

"A real man should be secure in his masculinity. He should be kind, know his duty, take responsibility for his actions, and be willing to make sacrifices for those he loves," said Tiberius, and she nodded.

"I know you don't really like my appearance as a man. But I enjoy having sex like that when you are a woman. It's indescribable and so much fun," said Val, and Tibs had to chuckle.

"I'm not trans or confused. I think I will always feel like a straight man, but the aliens have completely changed my perception of sex. I'm not being intimate with a man or a woman, but with Val, the person I love, and it's always amazing because I now know that you like it too."

"I don't like it; I love it," said Val and continued, "God, just talking about it arouses me again. You can't remember, but I told you once that I would still enjoy sex if you were an octopus. I think I really would."

"I bet I made an inappropriate comment when you said that," said Tiberius with a smirk as he drizzled some water on the lettuce.

"Of course, you naughty boy. You suggested that we try tentacle sex."

"Hmm, there is an idea..." said Tibs and snickered.

"No!" stated Val firmly, but then added mischievously, "Unless you want that, then yes, let's do it."

"What happened to the cold and calculating lesbian?" teased Tiberius.

"She died in a tar pit many years ago. Good riddance to her," said Val, adding softly, "I feel so safe with you. I don't need her anymore."

"Thanks, Val. That was possibly the nicest thing you ever said to me," said Tibs, looking at her fondly.

Valkyrie smiled back at him, but then she became earnest. For a moment, she didn't say anything while she was checking a planter. Eventually, she took a deep breath and spoke again.

"Tibs, I toyed with you when you were dying. I have lied, murdered, and betrayed you in the worst ways. Yet here you are, still kind, loving, and forgiving, and sticking with a reprehensible psycho," said Valkyrie and asked sternly, "What the hell is wrong with you?"

Since she had returned, Val was frequently haunted by guilt, but that wasn't anything Tiberius had modified in her mind. He suspected that she had developed those feelings independently of the edit. Of course, Tiberius had forgiven her and assured her that he harbored no grudge, but every so often, he had to do it again.

"I wish I knew how to quit you," said Tiberius, and smiled at her.

"Brokeback Mountain? Really?" quipped Val and rolled her eyes when she recognized the movie quote, and Tibs chuckled before he continued:

"You might not recall it, but the first time we met, you asked me how to stop thinking. Since then, I knew you were a fellow tortured soul, and that drew my attention."

"I remember it well. It was a cry for help; you answered it, and now you have another broken woman in your collection," said Val, revealing with a sigh, "When you banished me, I was hoping, wishing, and praying that you would contact me again someday. I thought I was having delusions when I saw your message."

"I was over the moon when you replied," admitted Tibs and raked one of the carrot patches.

"We are so wrong for each other, but nobody has been there for me like you have. Nobody has done even a fraction of what you have done for me. I don't deserve any of it, and I owe you more than just my life."

"You deserve all of it and owe me nothing. You are my needle, Val."

"For the first time in decades, I'm not restless. I'm able to think without my thoughts running amok. I still don't fully trust the new me, but I have hope now. Once again, you gave me a gift unlike any other."

"You are welcome, and I really hope it works," said Tibs, but Val didn't seem entirely convinced.

"Don't tell me what it is, but do you have a contingency plan if I go nuts again?"

"Hmm, you are my backup plan this time," said Tibs as he checked an irrigation valve.

"Explain that, please."

"If the edit fails and you revert to your old self, I'll let you win the game and kill me. Then you will celebrate your triumph in some wild and crazy fashion, but eventually, you will get bored again and resurrect me," said Tiberius, and added with a big grin, "And that's how I'll be victorious in the end."

"Damn! You know me too well," replied Val and giggled.

"Do you have the thoughts again?" he asked more seriously.

"No, none at all. Ever since you fixed me, it's been incredible. What exactly did you do?"

"The aliens used the mind edit to erase individuality. They considered that a flaw, and they had sophisticated tools to detect it. I used those tools to dampen certain memories and emotions and to heighten a few others, such as compassion. It was very precarious work, and I wasn't sure of the results."

"Thanks, Tibs. It works. It must," said Valkyrie as she was digging out a root.

"I didn't have an engagement ring, so messing with your mind was the next best thing," quipped Tibs.

"Engagement ring? Are you asking me to marry you?" wondered Val and smiled at him broadly.

"Would you marry me, Val?" asked Tiberius, looking at her expectantly.

"No," said Val bluntly, but added quickly, "A marriage could never come close to what we have."

"Now I'm hurt," said Tibs, and pouted a little.

"Fine, I do! I'm your wife now. Happy?" asked Val, putting her hands defiantly on her hips.

"Yes!" said Tibs and did a fist pump, while Val laughed out loud and then kissed him deeply.

"You once called me a master manipulator, and I freely admit to that. But you are on another level."

"How so?"

"Back on Earth, I would have laughed if anyone had told me that I would be in love with a man and marry him," said Valkyrie, shook her head, and continued softly, "Yet you managed to turn a murderous lesbian into your loving wife. Your persuasion skill is unmatched, Tibs."

"It was not my goal, and it would have never happened on Earth, but I'm happier than I've ever been in my life."

He kissed her, held her tightly in his arms, and smiled. They remained like that for a while, not saying a word. Eventually, she looked at him expectantly and stuck the spade into the ground.

"So, ready to consummate our marriage?"

"Out here?" wondered Tiberius and put his rake down as well.

"The tomatoes won't mind, baby," said Valkyrie in a sultry voice and reached for his groin.


Three months after Valkyrie's return, they had settled into their old routines, and it felt like Val had never left. She painted again, and Tibs was writing a new book on the flora and fauna of the planet. They laughed, they gardened, they danced, had lengthy discussions, and watched the stars every night, but the dynamics had fundamentally changed: instead of playing a deadly game,

Tiberius and Valkyrie had become a family. Val showed no signs of regression, but just in case, Tiberius backed up her personality and his own every day. Life was great, and the mischievous kittens only made it better.

Tibs was making breakfast every morning as he always did, but Val insisted on a slightly new ritual. When Tiberius handed her a coffee mug, he would ask her about her mental health. Val would reflect for a moment before giving her response.

"I love you, but I still prefer you as a woman, especially when you are that little geisha. I'm calm and happy and have no thoughts of killing you."

Tibs studied her carefully every time, but couldn't sense any deception. The alien mind edit was holding up, and both of them were elated about it. Today, the morning routine repeated, but Val's answer was unexpected:

"I love you. I'm calm and happy, but I consider killing you because you ruined my shapely figure."

For a second, Tiberius was concerned, fearing that the mental fix had finally worn off. But Val looked at him and grinned broadly. Perhaps she was just joking?

"What do you mean?" he asked carefully.

"For being a genius, you are really slow on the uptake sometimes."

"Huh?" asked Tiberius as he put the waffles in the toaster.

"I'm pregnant, you idiot!" stated Val loudly and rolled her eyes.

"Oh…" replied Tibs, his mouth agape and unable to say anything else.

Val was laughing hard. Then she put her coffee down, came behind the kitchen counter, and embraced him firmly.

"I'm so happy, Tibs."

"I love you, Val. What should I do? Do you need anything?" he stammered, not paying attention to the toaster.

"Yes, I need you. Now and always."

Tibs kissed her deeply, and she eagerly returned his affections. They hugged and kissed for several minutes in silence. Eventually, Tibs had to let go of her to remove the burnt waffles from the smoking appliance.

"That poor kid will be so screwed up with parents like us," quipped Tibs as he discarded the blackened food.

"No, because it will have the perfect dad," said Val, and smiled at him.

"And the perfect mother," added Tiberius and kissed her one more time.

"We are Adam and Eve in the Garden of Eden, and now we are the rebirth of humanity."

"Except we can't decide which one of us is either," replied Tibs and chuckled.

"True. But that's all the fun!" emphasized Val with a bright smile.

Then she hopped on the kitchen counter and put her arms around his neck. Tiberius held her waist and kissed her softly. Val opened her legs for him and closed them behind his back.

"This is how it all started," said Tibs quietly, remembering the first time they were intimate.

"Yes, but my feelings for you couldn't be more different this time," replied Val.

"Love conquers all," said Tiberius fondly.

Valkyrie didn't respond, but closed her eyes and gasped in delight as he entered her.

**THE END**

www.ingramcontent.com/pod-product-compliance
Lightning Source LLC
Chambersburg PA
CBHW071909220626
47052CB00002B/271